Oh, Mae, why do you make this all so hard?

Why couldn't she be the kind of woman who didn't have to be on the front lines of trouble? The one he'd known for a crazy, romantic week in Seattle?

Or maybe he hadn't known her at all.

She finally spoke, her words losing some of their heat, yet still stiff with anger. "If you knew anything about me, anything at all, Chet, you would know that I will not just go home and leave my teenage nephew here. I'm not built that way. I don't know what's going on with him—why he did this, or who this *princess* is—"

"She's the daughter of a warlord."

"Perfect. For all I know, he's being held against his will. But I made a promise to my sister. And I keep my promises."

He did know that about her.

He had four days to find a runaway princess and stop a love-struck teenager from starting an international incident, all while trying to keep up with the woman he most wanted to protect in the world.

Books by Susan May Warren

Love Inspired Suspense

Point of No Return

Steeple Hill

In Sheep's Clothing
Everything's Coming Up Josey
Sands of Time
Chill Out, Josey!
Wiser Than Serpents
Get Cozy, Josey!

*Missions of Mercy

SUSAN MAY WARREN

is the RITA® Award-winning, bestselling novelist of more than twenty-five novels, many of which have won an Inspirational Readers Choice Award, an ACFW Book of the Year award and been Christy and RITA® Award finalists. Her compelling plots and unforgettable characters have won her acclaim with readers and reviewers alike. She and her husband of twenty years, and their four children live in a small town on Minnesota's beautiful Lake Superior shore, where they are active in their local church. You can find her online at www.susanmaywarren.com.

POINT OF
NO RETURN

SUSAN MAY
WARREN

Steeple
Hill®

Published by Steeple Hill Books™

STEEPLE HILL BOOKS

Steeple Hill®

Recycling programs for this product may not exist in your area.

ISBN-13: 978-0-373-67445-9

POINT OF NO RETURN

Copyright © 2011 by Susan May Warren

www.SteepleHill.com

Printed in U.S.A.

When the man saw that he could not overpower him, he touched the socket of Jacob's hip so that his hip was wrenched as he wrestled with the man. Then the man said, "Let me go, for it is daybreak."

But Jacob replied, "I will not let you go unless you bless me."

The man asked him, "What is your name?"

"Jacob," he answered.

Then the man said, "Your name will no longer be Jacob, but Israel, because you have struggled with God and with men and have overcome."

—*Genesis* 32:25–28

A huge thank you to my family—Andrew, David, Sarah, Peter and Noah, and my secret weapon Ellen Tarver for helping me craft a book that I pray brings glory to the Lord.

PROLOGUE

Sometimes Chet Stryker could still feel Carissa's muddy grip slide from his. He could still see those brown eyes, stripped of all mystery, pleading with him, could still hear her scream echoing through the chambers of his brittle soul. Tonight, the memory twisted him inside his bedsheets, tightening like a constrictor around his legs, lacing his chest, noosing his breath. Sweat slicked his body, despite the rattle of the air conditioner pumping out breath against the sweltering, polluted Moscow air. He hiccupped, and with a cry that sounded more animal than human, he lurched into a sitting position, ripping himself from the dream, blinking against the darkness.

It wasn't real. *Not real.* Still, Chet pressed his hand to his bare chest, his heart jackhammering under his sternum, still smelling the cloying odor of bodies pressing him to the earth, his face ground against the loam of decaying leaves.

He closed his eyes, but of course, that only made

it worse. His mind too easily scraped up the image, now twenty years old, of Akif Bashim pushing Carissa to the dirt, holding her there. Hurting her, even as his Ossetian tribesmen made Chet watch.

Taking Chet's life apart, one blow after another.

"No!" He shook himself out of the nightmare and fumbled for the lamp, knocking over his water onto the carpet, his watch after it. The light switch slid under his sweat-slickened fingers, refusing to turn. He gave up, and for an agonizing, lost moment, fought with his tangled covers. Then, freeing himself, he lunged from the bed toward the bathroom.

He slapped on the light, braced his hands on the sink and simply breathed. One breath in, the next out. In. Out. Breathe.

He turned on the faucet, letting cold water trickle through his shaking fingers. Scooping it up, he splashed it on his face. The shock of the icy water against his skin loosened the last fingers of the dream from his mind, and he blew out another long breath. Stared into the mirror.

Water, caught in his overnight beard, glistened in the mean fluorescence, and his face seemed more brutal than he'd remembered. Or maybe he usually just refused to look too closely. He touched the spiderweb scar on his abdomen, running his fingers along the ridges, touching the hard knot of the scar tissue in the center. Sometimes he could still feel the instant, blinding burn of the bullet tearing through his flesh, see David's eyes flash with horror. Could hear his own teeth-grinding grunt as he crumpled onto the cement, hands clutched over his wound. Chet had let his partner shoot him without a whimper. Because that was what patriots did when asked to sacrifice for their country, especially while working undercover. At the time, the pain seemed a reasonable cost to help David keep his cover in a Chinese triad.

But no one had told him about the residual suffering, the ache and sometimes sudden, sharp pain. As if the wound still might be healing, deep inside, even after more than a year. Thankfully, most of the time, it just felt numb.

How he cherished numb.

He ran his fingers through the water again and rubbed a thumb and forefinger against his cracked, blue eyes. It eased the sting, albeit momentarily.

Turning off the water, he grabbed a towel and scrubbed his face, glancing again in the mirror. He needed a haircut—should have gotten one before today. His nearly black hair curled past his ears and down his back. It was no wonder Viktor's groomsmen David Curtiss and Roman Novik looked at him like something the dog dragged in.

He wanted to explain that he looked a lot better with the mess tied into a ponytail, that it was a look fashionable with his most recent clients, but now it only seemed a pronounced departure from his once-tidy military life.

Although it had been years since his life had actually resembled tidy.

Still, his cousin Gracie—the bride—deserved better from him. Maybe he'd have time to visit the local barber before the ceremony.

Reaching over, he turned on the shower, running his fingers through the trickles of ice, waiting for it to warm. Sleep would be impossible even if weren't foolhardy at this point.

The shower refused to cooperate, and he let the water spray as he walked over to the window, pushed aside the curtains and stared down from the sixth floor onto the street below. Its streetlamps pooled luminescence upon Neglinnaya Street, over a mix of ancient Ladas and new Mercedeses.

The sun had just begun to syrup through the cityscape, sliding between ancient buildings occupied by the former gentry of old Russia, gliding the turrets on the corner of the Kremlin walls, over the bright cupolas of St. Basil's Cathedral and lighting afire the iron troika perched atop the building across the street. Perhaps he'd go for a run. He liked Red Square in the morning, the slap of his feet against the red cobblestones of the parade grounds. Lately, he could even hear the ghosts of the Kremlin whispering, reminding him, in this new age, that the old conquerors still stirred.

Even his friend Viktor knew the past had begun to awaken. No wonder he wanted to escape Russia and move with his new bride to Prague, Czech Republic, to help start Chet's new security firm. It couldn't bode well for a former KGB agent to marry an American on the eve of a new cold war era.

Chet pressed his hand to the glass, wishing he could shake himself out of the dread that had kept him awake too many hours into the night.

He'd taken one look at Mae Lund at the rehearsal dinner, dressed in that green evening gown that shimmered under the indulgent moonlight of the terrace garden and turned her beautiful eyes to gems, her long, red hair to fire, and he knew he was in big trouble. He couldn't let her be a part of his new life.

Not if he wanted them both to survive.

He winced even as he imagined the conversation.

"No, Mae, I'm not hiring you."

"But, Chet, I'm the best pilot you have—"

"True."

"And I fly not only planes but helicopters, and I've flown in every kind of terrain."

"Again, true."

"And you're desperately in need of a great pilot for your international security team."

"Painfully true."

Then, in the agonizing silence, she'd look at him with those eyes that could make his stomach turn inside out and turn his mouth dry, and ask why.

And all he'd manage to growl out would be another cryptic *No*.

Because how could he tell her that it had taken him ten years to piece his life—his heart—back together after Carissa died?

Or that Mae had somehow put it back together?

Most of all, that he couldn't risk losing it again?

How could anyone expect Mae to sleep the night before her whole life would be transformed? Everything—her career, her home, even her identity—would change tomorrow.

A pilot for one of the premier security teams in the world. Her dream job.

Mae knew exactly how Gracie Benson, the bride-to-be, sleeping in the other double bed, might feel.

Well, maybe. It wasn't like Mae was getting

married, or even that Chet had the big M on his mind, but Mae had long ago pushed marital bliss from her list of reasonable, even desirable, life goals.

No. She wanted to fly.

And to do it for Chet's new company, Stryker International Security Management, the one he had just put together in Prague, Czech Republic.

Mae turned over onto her side, punched her pillow and stared at the ribbon of gray light streaming in through the dark velour curtains and across her mussed covers. He had to say yes. If anyone had been born for the job of transportation officer, it was Mae Lund, who'd spent twelve years in the Air National Guard, flying everything she could get her hands on. Somehow, when the army had stripped away her career—punishment for saving the life of an innocent man, which had included sneaking into Russia and hijacking a Russian chopper—they'd also stripped from her the reason to push herself out of bed every morning, and the strength to silence the voices of her childhood that prophesied failure.

Lately, she'd begun to listen.

Still, Mae had tried—given it all she had—to stave the desperation from her voice last night as she smiled at Chet and listed her qualifications.

As if he needed reminding. As if they hadn't

been corresponding for over a year, since they'd met at Gracie's birthday party in Seattle. As if he didn't know how flying for Seattle Air Scenic Tours slowly chipped away at her life, one sickeningly sweet, safe tour at a time. She could love the breathtaking beauty of the jagged mountain peaks of Mount Rainier, or the moonscaped lava dome of Mount Saint Helens, without embracing the hollowness of her everyday existence.

"Are you awake?"

The voice came from the other bed.

Shoot, the last thing Gracie needed on the early morning of her wedding was a restless roomie. "Sorry, am I keeping you awake?"

"Are you kidding? I'm keeping *you* awake."

Mae rolled over as Gracie sat up. Gracie looked wan and tired in the morning shadow. "You should have gotten a single room. Really. I'm so sorry."

"And miss out on early-morning girl talk? Never. Mind if I turn on the light?" Gracie reached for the lamp. "Truth is, I can't sleep."

"Stressed?" Mae sat up, rubbing her hands down her face.

"Excited. And worried. And excited. I can't believe we're finally getting married."

"And moving to Prague." Mae flopped back against the pillows, one arm over her head. "I love Prague. The clip-clop of horses' hooves on the cobblestone streets, the smell of the roses from the vendors in Old Town, the grandeur of Prague Castle, the gong of the Astronomical Clock echoing over the Charles Bridge."

"You make it sound romantic."

Mae would have termed it… "Resonant. Your life has to take on some sort of meaning amidst all that history. Think about it. Good King Wenceslas—you know, from the song?—lived there. It has outdoor markets and bistros…it's so… European."

"Please. Like we both don't know why you want to go there." Gracie grinned at Mae, pushed back her covers and climbed out of bed. "You'd move to the London slums, or better yet, war-torn Bosnia, if it meant you could fly choppers for Chet's new team."

Gracie had let her blond hair grow, and it now fell to her shoulders, shimmering in the sunlight as she parted the shades. Mae turned away from the brilliance even as Gracie peered down into the street. "He'll say yes. There's no one more qualified than you." Letting the curtain fall, she turned to Mae. "Besides, I think he has a little thing for you." She grabbed the complimentary robe and flung it over her shoulder. "I'm hopping in the shower."

Mae listened to the spray, to Gracie humming

behind the closed bathroom door, and stared again at the sliver of light, now growing more luminous. So, she had a little thing for him, too. Who wouldn't? With that unruly curly black hair and those wide shoulders, Chet had a reined-in recklessness about him that could whisk her breath from her. Probably, it only nudged her own tendency to live on the edge.

Still, she couldn't forget their one and only kiss, nearly a week after Gracie's birthday party over a year ago, right before he disappeared to Taiwan and another overseas assignment. She could still feel the press of his strong hands against her lower back. She could see the smile that had emerged, ever so briefly, from his dark blue hooded eyes.

A year of corresponding—especially when he'd been recuperating from the gunshot wound he'd received while on mission in Taiwan—had revealed a man devoted to his country. To his friends. To a life that she wanted, too. No, a life she needed.

She had no illusions—not really—that this thing between them might flourish into anything lasting. Not with her traumatic history and his tendency to throw himself in front of gunfire. But she did hope he'd see beyond that to her skills.

No, more than hoped.

Prayed for it with all she had in her.

Please, God, he had to say yes. Had to hire her as his new chopper pilot.

Because the alternative just might slowly suck the last of the marrow out of her already depleted life.

ONE

Times like this, Mae Lund thought she might actually hate Chet Stryker.

Mae stared at herself in the dingy mirror of the one-stall hangar bathroom, grimacing at the splotch of vomit-scented wetness that stained her jumpsuit. How she loved it when her scenic air tour passengers didn't follow instructions.

She should be flying C-130s for Chet Stryker's international security team. His voice still rang in her head. *I just don't want you to get hurt Mae—*

A pounding at the bathroom door made her jump. "Mae?" It was Darrin, her new, grumpy boss, annoyance in his tone that she'd stalked away from her nauseous tourists.

"Just a second!" She chucked another handful of paper towels into the trash and stripped off the jumpsuit. Still, her skin reeked of sickly-sweet, soap-imbued vomit. If her boss wanted her to go up again—

"Mae, get out here!"

"Hold your horses, I'll be right there!" She tugged on a pair of clean overalls over her tank top and pulled them up over her shoulders, then slipped on flip-flops. Scraping the edge off her voice, she reached for the door. "I just had to change. I can't believe that kid urped all over me. Can't his mother read the direc—"

Uh-oh.

Darrin stood before her, flanked by the dangerous urper and his mother. She gripped the kid around the waist as he sagged against her.

"They need to use the bathroom," Darrin said tightly.

They moved past her, the mother uttering a word that Mae would have edited for the kid's sake. The door clicked shut behind them, and Mae winced as she heard the splatter of another round of lunch.

"I'm not cleaning that up." Mae stared at Darrin—or, rather, stared down at Darrin and his bald spot. His furious little beady eyes made him appear more angry mole than former bush pilot.

"Rough ride?" Darrin took her by the elbow, pulling her away from the door. Mae glanced down at his hand and shot him a dark look.

"Not especially."

"She said that he wouldn't have gotten sick if you hadn't descended so quickly. And apparently there was also a steep climb—"

"Are you serious? It's a small plane, Darrin, not a jumbo jet. Airsickness is a probability, not just a remote possibility. You can't climb—or descend, for that matter—without feeling a little queasy. Why not ask them about the stop-off at McDonald's on the way to the airstrip? And, by the way, I didn't hear any complaints when I was buzzing them around the south crater."

So maybe…well, okay, she had been a little quick on the stick as they'd slid in and out of Olympic National Park, a favorite on the Seattle Air Scenic Tours schedule. But she'd wanted to give them a great view of the Carbon Glacier. Some people paid extra for that kind of flying.

Some people considered that kind of flying a talent. A work of art.

"This is the third complaint this month, Mae." Darrin pulled out a well-worn gimme cap from his back pocket and shoved it over his bald spot. He looked up at her and pursed his lips. "You're a good pilot, but you take too many risks—"

"What?" Risks? A risk was liberating a learjet from a serial killer and abandoning ship a second before it turned into fire and ash. Or hijacking a clunker chopper and flying under the radar into the icy winds of Siberia to save a buddy from execution. Okay, that one had cost her a thriving career with the military. "But really, I didn't risk anything—"

"You're risking my business. My livelihood." Darrin nodded to the mechanic wheeling the mop bucket out to the plane. "And I'm not the only one. Shall we count how many companies you've flown for in the past couple years?"

She looked over his head, through the hangar, out to where the sky was just purpling with the end of the day. She refused to wince as he listed them, one after another, in the nastiest tone he could muster. "You're out of options, lady. You either start flying smart, or you stop flying."

Stop flying. That was what it had come down to, hadn't it? Get a job serving coffee, or perhaps teaching—although she doubted any flight school would take her on, thanks to the closed ranks of the air charter services in Seattle.

She swallowed past the dread in her throat. "Sorry, Darrin."

"Now I gotta write up a refund. Go help clean up the plane." He turned and stalked back to his office.

Perfect. She'd gone from decorated rescue pilot to cleaning crew.

That was what she got for putting her dreams into the hands of Chet Stryker.

She met the mechanic rolling his mop bucket back inside. "All cleaned, Mae."

"Thanks." Time for a quick escape. She jogged out to her ten-year-old Montero, which felt like a sauna after sitting in the summer sun all day, and rolled down the windows. The stereo came on full blast, and she twisted the knob to Off before Darrin could hear her fleeing.

Pulling out, she spotted him emerging from the hangar and ignored his frantic waving. She angled her elbow out the window as she exited the air-field, noticing a beautiful Piper Cub from the local aviation school touching down. And beyond that a gleaming helicopter sat on the pad. Most pilots weren't rated on both aircraft and helicopters, but she'd taken her chopper exam for her stint in ocean rescue.

Frankly, she didn't care what she flew. Just as long as she could escape into the heavens. She slammed her hand on the steering wheel, then turned on the radio. Screamer music. Loud. Pulsing. Perfectly impossible to think at this decibel.

Nearly impossible, also, to hear her cell phone nestled in the cup holder between her seats. Had she not glanced down at the stoplight and seen it vibrating inside its silver skin, she would have missed the call altogether.

She turned the radio down and grabbed the cell, flipping it open. "Mae here."

Oh, why hadn't she checked the display? "Mae Lund, you turn your car around this second or don't bother showing up here again." Mae shut her phone. Nope, no job tomorrow.

The phone vibrated again in her grip, and this time she checked the display.

Lissa.

What now? She flipped the phone open and didn't bother to check her tone. "What, Lissa?"

"Mae?" The voice on the other end wobbled.

Mae bit back a *"Whose phone do you think you're calling?"* and opted for something softer. After all, her kid half-sister didn't mean to be Mae's polar opposite— timid, pliable, fragile. That blame Mae reserved for their mother.

"It's me, Lis."

Mae heard silence, or perhaps a gasp of breath— still, the hiccupping sound was enough for Mae to pull over. She turned into a Dunkin' Donuts and switched ears. "What's up, honey?"

Sometimes—well, most of the time—it was hard to believe that Lissa, only two years younger than Mae, had a college-age son, given the way Lissa so often resembled a thirteen-year-old in the throes of a temper tantrum. Then again, she'd been just a little more than thirteen when she had little Joshy.

Little Joshy. Perhaps Mae should stop thinking of the nineteen-year-old by the nickname she'd given him when he'd run through their trailer in a saggy, wet diaper.

"What is it, Lis?" Mae pulled the ponytail holder out of her hair and wrapped it around her wrist, running her fingers through her sweaty mane.

"It's...it's Josh."

Mae switched ears again with the phone, rolling up the window to cut out street noise. "What's wrong with Josh?"

"He's...missing, Mae."

Huh? "Wasn't he going camping or something?" Josh had called earlier in the summer, right after his freshman year at Arizona State, excited because he'd hooked up a summer internship with some medical group. "No, he was going to work for Ambassadors of Health, right?"

"Yeah, and they sent him to Georgia."

Mae had been to Georgia few times. "Maybe he and few friends just took off, went camping somewhere along the Appalachian Trail. He said he was bringing that backpack I got him for graduation—"

"No! No, Mae, listen. Not Georgia. *Georgia. The country.*"

Mae's gaze focused on a woman and a young boy emerging from the doughnut shop as she tried to process Lissa's words in her head. In the heat of the closed car, her own odor watered her eyes. "Georgia, as in *former-satellite-of-the-Soviet-Union* Georgia?"

"Yes." Her word caught on a sob.

"Georgia? North of Iraq, next to Pakistan, Georgia? The one that recently got *invaded by Russia?*" Mae opened the door and got out, gulping in fresh air. "Why is he in *Georgia?*"

"That's where the aid group sent him. They went over to work in a clinic. Give vaccinations and checkups or something. He was supposed to be there for a month—the rest of his team came home last week—but he wanted to stay. I thought it would be okay, but I just got a call from his leaders, and yesterday he vanished. Maybe he ran off, or maybe…maybe…"

"Kidnapped." Mae pushed her sweaty hair away from her face as she turned toward the road. Cars clogged at the stoplight, the rhythmic beat of a radio spilling into the chaos. Pedestrians hurried across the crosswalk, most with cell phones pressed to their ears. A dog barked at her from the cracked window of a banged-up caravan.

But for Mae, everything had gone still. "Kidnapped," she whispered again.

Lissa's communication had been reduced to muffled crying.

Mae knew the price of an American teenager in a foreign land—for any American, really, but a kid, now that amounted to a jackpot for any terrorist group looking to cash in. Only this time, they'd picked the wrong kid. A poor kid. A kid without rich parents.

Her kid.

"Find him, Mae. I know you…you have friends in the military—what about those friends from Russia? Or your old roommate? Didn't she marry someone from Russia? Or maybe that American soldier—what was his name—?"

"David."

"Yeah, him." Hope quickened Lissa's voice. "He might know something. Or maybe you could ask that boyfriend in Europe?"

"Chet." Mae's throat burned even as she dredged out his name. "Chet runs an international security company."

"Yes, Chet! Aren't you two dating?"

"We *were* dating, a long time ago, Lis. Good grief, don't you listen to anything I say?"

Silence on the other end, followed by an indrawn, even shaky breath, made Mae cringe. "We broke up a year ago but that doesn't matter." She opened her car door and slid back in. "I'll find him, Lis. I'll find Joshy."

When Lissa spoke again, Mae heard the confidence, the trust that she'd always found so painfully suffocating—and today, terrifying. "I know you will, Mae."

Mae hung up. Stared at the phone. Shoot. She hated this part.

I love you, Mae. But I don't want you to work for me.

You mean you don't want me in your life, she'd said.

She would never forget his steady, dark-eyed stare, or the rawness in his expression.

Nor the hurt on his face when she'd dumped her drink over his head and walked away.

She only gave herself another moment's debate before breaking all her promises to herself and dialing the man who'd nose-dived her life.

Her heart.

Chet Stryker.

As with every mission Chet Stryker had ever accepted, he did his homework, armed himself with the latest technology, contemplated every strategy and embraced whatever character his assignment demanded.

"I really hate tulle," he said, as he exited through

the security gates of Hans Brumegaarden's expansive estate in his Snow White costume. The sun had long ago abandoned the day, and a sprinkling of stars barely outshone the lights of Berlin.

"It does tend to snag on your ankle holster," Brody "Wick" Wickham said, hoisting his overnight bag of supplies—ammunition, a Heckler and Koch submachine gun, a couple of Glocks and various high-tech surveillance equipment—over his shoulder, his bad mood etched on his craggy face. "I could use a night at the Hyatt."

Chet didn't blame him. His elite security team had spent five hours in the late summer sun dressed as Grumpy, Sleepy and Sneezy. Lucky him, as the team leader, Chet had landed the role of Snow White.

He had to be the laughingstock of the international-security community. Apparently, if anyone needed a decorated, former Delta Force operative with ten years of undercover experience and his team of highly trained specialists to impersonate fairy-tale characters, Chet Stryker was their man.

He'd wanted to run Stryker International on his terms. With his choice of assignments.

But clearly pride wouldn't pay the bills. And they had accomplished their mission—to protect six-year-old Gretchen Brumegaarden and one hundred of her closest friends and family members from a terrorist threat. Still, it felt like a compromise. He needed to do everything he could to make his little company a success, hoping to convince himself that he hadn't blown everything when he'd retired early from the military.

Since the day he'd kicked Mae out of his life, it seemed he'd made one glaring mistake after another.

"We're taking the midnight train back to Prague," Chet said, pressing the automatic unlock on their economy rental car.

"No airplane?" Artyom, his computer techie from Russia, ran to catch up, toting his own provisions, most of them contained in his laptop case. He'd been recruited by Wick, a former Green Beret whom Chet had enticed to leave special ops after a particularly brutal tour. Chet's business partner Vicktor—a former FSB agent—had closed the deal, talking Artyom into joining Stryker International. Luke Dekker, former Navy SEAL, acted as medic and team explosives expert. Now all Chet needed was a profiler, perhaps a negotiator, and, yes, a pilot.

He still hadn't found someone as skilled as Mae. Not even close. He'd been setting his sights lower and lower, until he was looking at recruits fresh out of a bush pilot school in Alaska. He needed

Mae. But every time he opened his phone to call her, his chest would burn, old wounds stirring to life, and he'd shut his phone and the image of her from his mind.

He wouldn't—couldn't—put someone he loved in the line of fire. Been there, done that.

Chet opened the trunk and threw in the gear. "No airplane. This check barely covers our expenses and salaries for the next month. An airplane means another dwarf suit in your near future."

Chet needed a break, something to put his business on the map. Something big, international and newsworthy.

Maybe even something to make him feel like a soldier, a patriot, again. Anything but a cartoon character playing a charade.

The wind blew against the ancient elm trees ringing the property, picking up his rather un-Snow-White scent. "Let's get out of here."

His cell phone vibrated as he opened the car door. Fishing it out of his pocket, he looked at the number—and stilled.

"You drive, Wick." Chet tossed him the keys, walked over to the passenger side and opened the phone. "Chet here."

"It's…me."

"I know." Wow, did he know, because just like that, everything he'd felt that day when he'd met Mae Lund—the longing, the hope, even the delight—rushed back and took a swipe at his voice. He found it, although it emerged a little roughed up as he turned from the car. "How are you, Mae?"

"Not so good." Was there a tremor in her voice?

"What is it?"

"It's my nephew, Josh. He's missing."

"Then call the police."

"He's in Georgia."

"I'm not sure what I can do from here—"

"Georgia, the country!" Her voice resounded loud and clear, and on the edge of desperate, despite being on the other side of the world. Uh, she *was* on the other side of the world, right? "Where are you?"

"Getting on a plane in Seattle."

"Let me guess—to Prague."

Silence. Then, "No, to Georgia. Why would I come to Prague?"

Wow, *that* hurt, more than he would have ever guessed. Because for a second he'd been hoping, wildly perhaps, that she'd forgotten how he'd stomped her pride into tiny bits, and instead remembered that once upon a time he really cared what happened to her. What she thought about. What food she liked and what movies she saw. What her dreams were...outside the ones that

included the rather negative byproduct of him
watching her die, that was.

"You're going to *Georgia?*"

"Where else would I be going, Chet? Honolulu?
My nephew is missing, and I speak Russian, which
means I can probably get by, thanks to the years
of Russia occupation. My sister is losing her mind,
and I think I can find him. I know he was working
near Gari…in a village called Burmansk." Her
voice dropped. "I was hoping that…maybe…oh…
never mind."

"Wait!" *Don't hang up.* "You want me to find
him?"

"No. I can find him. I was hoping you could
tap into your contacts in Georgia to help me." Her
voice dropped. "You know the ones."

"Yes, I know the ones." He climbed into the car
as Wick started it up and cranked the air conditioner. "I'd forgotten that I'd told—"

"I didn't." She said it softly, as if the details of
the letters he'd written while he'd been in Taiwan
had mattered to her. Only she didn't know it all
because if she did she would never have called,
would never have asked him to dig into his past.

"I…I'm not sure that's such a great idea, Mae.
don't even know if I can find the right people any
more." Not to mention the bounty on his head in
that particular country. Mae could be walking righ

into the fallout that he'd always dreaded. "Have you called the embassy?"

"Yes, but their official position is that Josh ran away with a local village girl."

"Maybe he did."

"He's not that irresponsible. He calls home every Sunday night, and was the only kid in his Sunday school who earned a gold star for perfect attendance. He's an Eagle Scout, for Pete's sake. He's not going to just take off and scare everyone around him!"

"Calm down, Mae. I'm sure he's already back."

"He's not back, Chet, that's the point!"

"But it doesn't mean you should go running off to Georgia! There's still a war going on over there!"

"Exactly why we need to find him. What if he's been kidnapped?"

"What if *you* get kidnapped?" He took a breath and lowered his voice to something that resembled calm. "What if something happens to you?"

"Nothing's going to happen to me."

But it would; he knew it in his gut. He'd seen the civil war between Georgia and Ossetia up close, and with Russia as Ossetia's new comrades, one nasty misfire from the Georgian side and the entire mess could reignite. Just give the Ossetians one reason, and no amount of international tongue-clucking would keep them from unloading their Kalashnikovs right into the rag-tag Georgian defenses.

And Mae would be caught in the middle, a beautiful redheaded American pawn, leverage for whatever terrorist group nabbed her.

"Please don't go, Mae. It's not safe—"

"Last time I checked, I didn't need your approval. You're not my boss."

He clenched his jaw so tight he thought his molars might crack. "I can't believe you're doing this again! Have you learned nothing about acting on impulse?"

He realized he was shouting when Wick glanced at him. He exhaled slowly as they turned onto Karl Liebknecht Street. The architecture in this part of old Berlin betrayed the age of the city—the dangling chandeliers that lined the streets, the colonnades of the stately former Third Reich buildings, the grandeur of the Brandenburg Gate, now silent and looming over them. "I'm sorry, Mae, that wasn't fair—"

"You bet it wasn't. If I hadn't 'acted on impulse' and helped spring Roman out of prison, he might still be there. Or maybe not—maybe he'd be *dead*. I know that he wasn't *your* friend, but, well, I guess it's clear that even if he had been, you wouldn't have lifted a finger to—"

"Watch yourself, Mae."

"Forget I called. Just forget it, Chet." The phone went dead before Chet could open his mouth.

He closed the phone, holding it in his shaking fist, gritting his teeth.

"Maybe you'll feel better if you throw it," Wick said quietly.

"I knew a woman like that once," Luke said from the backseat. "Drove me crazy."

"I married one," Artyom added.

Chet shook his head, staring out the window. Crazy was going to Georgia to search for a teenager who'd probably decided to backpack around Europe. Or better yet, hooked up with a village girl and disappeared for a weekend tryst.

"She's going to Georgia."

"Isn't that where you—"

"Yep," Chet snapped, cutting Wick off.

"Where what?" Artyom asked, leaning forward in the seat.

Wick glanced at Chet, and when he didn't answer, filled in the silence. "When he was a young Green Beret, Chet embedded with a group of rebels in the breakaway territory of Ossetia and helped them with equipment and supplies—"

"I helped them start a civil war." Among other things. His own words had the precision of a scalpel, the old wounds fresh and raw. His palms slicked. Carissa's scream still echoed through the chambers of his brittle soul. He shook himself from the memory, wiping his hands on his knees.

"He did more than that," Wick said. "The leaders in Georgia declared him an enemy of the state and put a price on his head. If he ever goes back to Georgia—"

"Unofficially, I'm also wanted in the territory of Ossetia—the one that recently conspired with the Russians to invade Georgia—by a terrorist group called the Svan. Their leader, Akif Bashim, would like nothing better than to find me, and throw in a little torture—just for payback—before he beheads me, of course." Deep breaths, in, out... Chet tapped the phone on his leg.

"I don't understand—if you helped the Svan, and Akif was their leader, why would he want you dead?"

Chet shook his head. *Leave it, Wick.*

Wick's eyes narrowed just a second before he betrayed him. "Let's just say that Akif had a daughter, who fell in love with Chet."

Chet drew in a breath. "Yes, something like that."

Wick reached over and tugged the cell from his whitened grip, dropping it into the cup holder. "Mae will be fine."

"She won't be fine." Chet flexed his hands. "But

if I set foot in that part of the world, Bashim will know it. And neither of us will get out of Georgia alive."

"You can't go, boss," Luke said quietly.

Chet leaned his head back against his seat, closing his eyes, and almost instantly Mae appeared, her green eyes bright, her red hair ribboning down her back, her skin sweet and tangy, her soft laughter like a balm on his calloused heart, smiling as he waltzed her around the dance floor of Viktor and Gracie's wedding reception. Their last magical moment.

Before she dumped the drink over his head.

He ran his finger and thumb over his eyes, dispelling the image. "But can I live with myself if I don't?"

TWO

Chet blamed his stupidity on his fatigue and the fact that he'd spent twelve hours on a train staring at the ceiling of his sterile compartment, listening to Wick snore, and trying not to imagine Mae disembarking in the Georgia airport in Tbilisi to Russian gunpoint.

No, he'd thought he was overreacting. The gun pointing wouldn't start until she got to Gori and met one of the trigger-nervous eighteen-year-old Russian "brown boys" supposedly "peacekeeping" along the Ossetia-Georgian border. He'd read the papers over the past few months. "Peacekeeping" seemed to be a euphemism for "daily terrorist attacks." These days, regions of Georgia bore a strong resemblance to some areas of Iraq.

And hadn't that been a comforting thought at 2:00 a.m. as they'd crossed the Berlin border into the Czech Republic? Chet had found himself staring out the window at the dark, rolling countryside of Europe, seeing instead the sweeping hills of Ossetia, rimmed by the jagged, snowy peaks of the Caucasus Mountains to the north. Ageless villages, nestled in the nooks and crannies of mountains lush with fir trees, each centered on a lone, stone church. He could nearly smell the lamb kebobs roasting over an open pit, or baking *Khachapuri,* dripping with cheese. He could hear children laughing as they bicycled through the village, just outside his window, open to the spring air.

But every memory of Georgia ended with the staccato roll of a Kalashnikov being chambered.

He'd closed his eyes, breathing out the past.

No, sleep, regardless of how inviting, hadn't been a great idea. Not if he ended up rolling in his sheets, lathered in a cold sweat, screaming. Just what Wick and the rest of his team needed for inspiration.

Instead, Chet had focused on figuring out a way to get into Georgia, sans capture, track down Mae and talk her—or throw her—out of the country.

No wonder he hadn't gotten any sleep on that train. And no wonder, when he'd shoved his key into his office headquarters, he didn't realize that the security system hadn't beeped. He'd just pushed his way inside the sparse and dreary three-room flat, dropped his gear on the checkerboard red and black floor, and reached for the light.

It shed the barest luminescence over his dismal office. He'd turned a fifteenth-century, three-room residence into his headquarters. The largest room, flanked by two ornate French doors, housing his black prefab desk, his computer, a couple of black faux-leather chairs and a huge window that over-looked a grassless courtyard, served as his recep-tion and office area.

In a room the size of his former walk-in closet in D.C., he'd fashioned a kitchen of sorts. It over-looked the alley, held a mini-fridge and a one-burner hotplate, and did a nearly miraculous job of infusing everything in the kitchen with the smell from the corner dumpster below. It was with relief that he did his dishes in the bathtub.

The last room housed their equipment, a veri-table stash of electronics, and enough weaponry to take over a small, unarmed country. Oh, and his single bed. And a hanging rack for his clothes.

And, he noticed too late, the CIA.

The two suits, with their high and tight crew cuts and clean-shaven chins, must have lost some shut-eye themselves on the flight over from the Pentagon, because they barely cleared their hol-sters before Chet walked in on them, rubbing his eyes and hoping to flop down on his bed.

"What the—"

And that was all he got out before he, too, had

his Glock in his hand, pointed at the taller of the two spooks, a guy who looked as if he might have played defensive end for Ole Miss, complete with the square jaw and blue-eyed stare.

They all breathed a long moment before Ole Miss lowered his weapon. He glanced at his pal. "Agents Miller and Carlson. We just want to talk."

"Talk without the guns," Chet said, his voice deadpan, all vestiges of fatigue flushed from his system.

Carlson lowered his weapon, tucking it back into his arm holster. "We're the good guys, remember?" A smirk tugged at his mouth as his brown eyes ran over Chet.

Yeah, good guys. He'd been a "good guy" for a different organization once upon a time. He wasn't sure there was such a thing anymore.

Chet lowered his Glock. "What do you want?"

"We have a situation and we need your help." This from Ole Miss, who backed away and sat on Chet's bed, right on the sleeping bag. He folded his hands and smiled, like, *Calm down, pal, everybody's friends here.*

Chet didn't put his gun away. "I'm tired, guys, so make it snappy. What situation?"

Carlson glanced at Miller and nodded. Miller reached for a briefcase that Chet was now noticing about thirty seconds too late. If it had been a bomb, well, so much for worrying about what Disney character to play in his next gig.

Miller pulled out a folder and handed it to Chet.

Chet took it, his gaze still on the spooks. "Why don't we talk in my office?" He gestured with a nod toward the front room, then stepped back to follow his guests.

He opened the folder on the way.

The girl in the photo staring back at him couldn't have been more than sixteen. Huge blue eyes, regal cheekbones, long sable hair that framed her face in thick waves. She wore a red *jilbab* ornamental dress, and in an inset photo, accompanied it with a silky white *hijab*. She looked very familiar. Painfully familiar. No, it couldn't be.

"Who is she?" Chet asked as he dropped the file onto his desk. Miller and Carlson had already folded themselves into the chairs.

"She's a princess. A Svan princess." Miller said.

A knot tightened low in Chet's gut. "Please don't tell me—"

"She's the daughter of Akif Bashim."

Chet closed his eyes, running his hand over them. Of course. She was the spitting image of Carissa. "Who is she?"

"Her name is Darya. Do you know her?"

No. But she could have been a young Carissa at sixteen, except for the eyes. Chet eased himself into a chair. "I'm too tired for games. Just lay it out there."

"She's been kidnapped. Or maybe something else. Intel's a little sketchy. But we need you to find her."

Chet was too raw to play it cool, too tired to even be curious about why the CIA had darkened *his* door to dangle this mission before him.

"When? How?"

"Yesterday. West of Gori, in the state of Georgia," Carlson said.

Chet closed one eye to stave off the stabbing sensation in his brain. Clearly the cosmos, or perhaps providence, didn't want to give him a break.

"We think she was taken by an aid worker from one of the refugee camps."

Chet turned another page and stared at what could only be Mae's nephew. Joshy? He recognized a hint of trouble in the kid's green eyes, in the angled set of his jaw. Great. Two stubborn redheads running around Georgia for him to rescue.

"American?" Chet didn't want to give too much away, just in case the CIA *wasn't* tapping his cell phone.

"From Arizona, on a do-gooder trip. He's

nineteen. He's been there for a month, working with some local mission group. We're not sure how he met Bashim's daughter, but they were last seen walking away together from the refugee camp."

Miller leaned forward and turned the next page for Chet, revealing a map of the hot zones inside Georgia, demarcating troop movements on both sides of the no-man's land. Gori sat smack in the middle. "I don't have to tell you that we're sitting on an international incident here, Stryker. Bashim hasn't been easy to nail down over the past few years, and more than a few intel sources suggest he's behind the Ossetia rebel forces."

"I thought he'd moved to Chechnya."

"We haven't had an official sighting since, well, since you and your team moved out, really. We had an insider source who kept track of him until a few years ago. Since then, he's gone dark."

Chet said nothing, made no comment on their knowledge of his history. He just turned the page. Yep, there was Bashim, bearded, yellow teeth, his head swaddled in a tight black turban. Chet's hand began to tremble.

"You know why we picked you, Stryker?"

Chet nodded as he looked up and closed the folder. "But I'll only make it worse."

"You're the only one who can do this. You know the territory, the languages—"

"It's been a while since I've spoken Georgian—"

"Then study up. Most important, you understand why you must find this girl. The agency will make it worth your while—not only now, but later, too."

Chet glared at them, hating how they knew so much—and the way they knew just how to use it.

Miller leaned forward, lowering his voice. "And if Darya did run away on her own power, you gotta talk her into going back home."

Chet stared at him, fighting the urge to launch himself across the desk, take the man by his burly neck and have a go—frankly, it might make him feel better, flush out all this simmering frustration. Or perhaps, instead, he should fling the file off his desk and watch the papers scatter into the air, not unlike his life so many years ago. He was still working on scraping up the pieces.

"Has it occurred to either of you geniuses that she's better off? Life at home in Bashim's camp isn't exactly peaches. Who knows what she's had to endure, living on the run in the mountains of northern Georgia with terrorists?"

"She's a student at Oxford."

"She looks like a kid."

"That was taken a few years ago, obviously." Carlson got up, paced to Chet's window and peered down at the courtyard. "She was in Western culture long enough to know just what her father is up to, and what it could mean for the world." He turned to Chet, arms folded. "She's betrothed to Akeem Al-Jabar."

The agent waited as if that name might ring a bell for Chet.

"I'm too tired—"

"Iranian prince. Son of Osama Al-Jabar."

Oh. Of course. "The same oil tycoon who's behind the truckloads of cash being poured into Iran's nuclear program."

"You do read the international news wires, then."

"When I'm not catching up on *Reader's Digest.* Just so I can connect the dots, Darya is educated, and I'm assuming since you know her political disposition—you, meaning the collective CIA—"

"And others."

"Right. And *others,* have coerced—" he particularly enjoyed watching Carlson flinch "—her into a forced marriage so she can, what, spy on the Iranians for you?"

Carlson turned back to the window. Miller pursed his lips, staring at Chet.

"Great. So now I'm a matchmaking service. Let me get my wand." He pushed back from the chair and stood. "I don't know what you're thinking, guys, but I'm not going to track down a runaway girl and drag her back by her hair like some caveman so I can throw her into marital slavery. Sorry, but I gotta draw the line somewhere."

"I know you won't draw the line at dressing like Snow White, but saving the world from nuclear holocaust puts you over the edge?"

Chet scooped up the folder and held it out. "Personally, I'm against human trafficking in all forms. You should have discovered that in your homework somewhere." Before he started his company, he'd spent five years—and earned one spider-webbed scar low in his gut—bringing down a Chinese human trafficking ring. His last great mission.

He stared at Carlson, then Miller. "I can't help you boys."

Miller stood and took the folder. "That's a real shame, because I hear that Bashim already has a price out for the kid who took her." He met Chet's eyes, speaking slowly. "And anyone caught aiding and abetting him."

So they *had* been tapping his phone.

"Listen, Stryker," Carlson said quietly. "Darya agreed to the marriage. In fact, she came to us with the idea of marrying Al-Jabar. They're friends from London. We're not the thugs you've drawn in your mind."

"She ran away for a reason."

"She's nineteen. She got cold feet. Or maybe she has a thing for this kid. We don't exactly know, but until someone finds them, Bashim is a powder keg. He gets itchy and invades Georgia again, and suddenly we have an international incident. Georgia fights back, Russia roars in to protect Ossetia, and with Georgia on track to be a member of NATO, well, who knows how far this thing could reach," said Miller.

Translation: American troops on the front lines of another war.

"And, as Miller pointed out, this thing touches home for you in many ways, doesn't it?"

Chet wasn't sure what they might be referring to. Yes, he'd spent his years early in his career arming the Ossetian rebels, namely Akif Bashim and his tribesmen, for freedom during their civil war. Back in the late eighties, the powers that be had simply wanted Ossetia to break free of Russia's grip, via the Republic of Georgia. But he held no allegiances to Ossetia—especially since, twenty years later, they had banded with the Russians to attack Georgia. Maybe Miller referred to Chet's hope of revenge and the opportunity to see Bashim pay for murdering the woman Chet was tasked to protect. Or perhaps he referred to rescuing Mae Lund, the woman he couldn't forget—didn't want to forget—who was now flying right into the danger zone of southern Georgia without a clue about the hornet's nest awaiting her.

He sighed.

Miller tossed the file back on the desk. "There's a visa and your flight pass. Hope you don't mind flying military. It'll be just like old times."

Oh, joy, the chilly back end of a C-130. He hoped he still had his earplugs.

Carlson followed Miller out. "According to our sources, you've got five days until the groom arrives. Try not to be late for the wedding."

It didn't matter what former Soviet satellite country Mae stepped into—it all smelled, sounded and felt like Moscow.

It wasn't a fair assessment, and Mae knew it— after all, Ukraine had worked hard to shed the residue of Russian imperialism the minute the iron curtain fell. Mae well remembered the crowds toppling the iron statues of Lenin along Khreschatyk Street. And Latvia and Estonia fought for their freedom years before they actually saw the Russian tanks heading for the border.

But despite the battles for freedom, Russia had stamped her architectural and cultural fingerprint onto the satellite societies so indelibly that, as Mae climbed up from the subway line to the center of

Tbilisi, Georgia, time swept her back to her days at Moscow University.

From the names of the streets—Lenin Square, of course, and Komsolmolskaya Street—to the statuesque cement buildings with their narrow wrought-iron balconies and street vendors lined up selling shiny gold religious icons, sunflower seeds, walnuts and bright pink peonies…she could be standing in the shadow of the Kremlin. She half expected to see her old college Russian pals, Roman and Vicktor, emerge from under the red umbrella of a food vendor, holding a dripping *plumbere* ice-cream cone.

In a wide fountain at the end of the square, children splashed, water dribbling off the backs of their drawers as they shivered in the early fall air. A yellow trolleybus rattled by, sparks jumping off the overhead electric line. Mae's stomach rolled over at the aroma of grilled mutton—*shashlik*, probably—but all she spotted was a scarf-headed babushka in a doughy apron sitting beside a tin milk can hawking *chebureki*—deep-fried meat sandwiches. She'd exchanged money at the airport and now held out a bill, waving off the change as the woman handed her the bread wrapped in grease-dotted paper.

She bit into it, letting the grease drip out onto

the sidewalk, and familiarity soothed her ragged nerves as she focused on her next steps.

She hadn't eaten since the airport in New York, about a thousand years ago.

A thousand years, four airplanes, and three hours in passport control. Thankfully, she still had some connections, the kind that could nab her a humanitarian-aid visa in twenty-four hours, which she picked up in Amsterdam. She owed pal and embassy officer in Russia David Curtiss again, for his quiet trust in her, as well as his string-pulling.

She refused to even allow Chet's reaction to her trip into the no-fly zone to enter her thoughts. *Have you learned nothing about acting on impulse?*

Hey, impulse saved lives. Sometimes impulse was all a girl had.

Although impulse was exactly how she'd ended up getting her heart broken with Chet. Maybe he had a point.

She used to be some sort of army pilot—they said she could fly just about anything. Too bad she threw away her career. Now she's waiting tables...

She heard the voice in her head and tried to shake it away, remembering now how she'd stood at the threshold of the sliding-glass door to the balcony of Gracie's apartment two years ago listening to three know-it-all teenagers from the youth group Gracie worked with summing up her life. Or rather, the life of the "hot redhead who lives with Gracie." She'd nearly crammed the serving plate full of cream-cheese roll-ups she'd been about to bring them down their throats.

She appreciated the fact those words hadn't issued from the military type who'd come to Gracie's birthday party dressed in a pair of jeans and a suit coat, the one who stood for ten minutes by the door, sizing up the room as if searching for terrorists, before wandering out to the balcony.

Mae still hadn't gotten his name and hated that her gaze had lingered on him, taking in his dark blue eyes, curly, short dark hair and wide shoulders. He stuck one hand into his front jeans pocket—a casual pose—but every inch of him radiated a sort of coiled tension, as if at the slightest provocation, he might morph into Jason Bourne or Jack Bauer.

He stood apart from the teens, clearly listening and forming his own opinion as one of those dark eyebrows arched up.

Mae shouldered right into the group, ignored the openmouthed expressions of her accusers, and shoved the plate at the chief hanging judge, a pimply kid no more than seventeen with wide eyes peeking through a shank of unwashed hair. "Care for a cream-cheese roll-up? Gotta earn my tips, after all."

He blanched, and with a shaky hand reached for the appetizer.

"Be glad you don't pull back a nub, son," the quiet man said from just behind him. Mae narrowed her eyes at his slight smirk, then turned on her heel, ready to bail.

So it was her new roommate's birthday party. So what if one of Gracie's best friends from Russia had shown up. Last time Mae had checked her status, she was jobless, her former squeeze—Vicktor—was engaged to said roommate, and now she had a bunch of teenagers laughing at her and her dismal life. And to make it worse, as she returned to Gracie's squatty galley kitchen, yet another teenager from Gracie's youth group streaked out and hit the plate, which flew from Mae's grip.

"Clearly, you're not a waitress." She whirled and Special Ops from the balcony held up his hands in surrender. "Not a criticism. Just an observation." He bent down and began to gather up the debris.

"No, I'm not," she finally said, as he stood and handed her the plate. "I'm a pilot."

"And according to my former partner David, a good one."

And then he smiled.

Beautiful. Lethal. She actually felt her heart stop.

"Chet Stryker. Gracie's cousin."

And the Delta Force pal of one of her best friends, David Curtiss.

Oh, she knew how to pick 'em.

She smiled and stuck out her hand. "Mae Lund. Former pilot and current catastrophe."

She meant it as a joke, but even as the words came out, they felt so raw, so fresh, that stupid tears raked her eyes.

She turned away before he could see.

But he had, because he touched her arm. "Don't listen to those kids. They don't know the facts like I do. You saved a friend from execution, even if you had to break a couple international laws to do it—that's worth waiting tables, I think."

She closed her eyes. Yes. Yes, it was.

He turned her, gently. "Hey, we all make choices we regret. Even if they're the right ones." He pushed her long red hair from her eyes, tucking it around her ear. "C'mon. Let's get out of here. I promise to take good care of you."

Such good care that a year later, knowing what it meant to her, he refused to give Mae a job flying for Stryker International.

Sometimes she just wished for a man who wasn't quite so…protective.

Except it wasn't as if Chet had come rushing to Tbilsi, was it? Apparently Chet had really meant it when he said he didn't want her on his team. He didn't even want to be associated with her.

It didn't matter. She was so over Chet Stryker. Over him and his swagger and his overprotective urges and his devastating smile. O-*ver*.

She'd find Joshy on her own.

She wadded the greasy paper and sandwich into a ball and threw it into a trash can, no longer hungry.

Now that she was here, she'd start by checking in with the powers that be—namely, the American Embassy—and see if they might point her in the right direction.

She'd looked up the address online at a kiosk in Amsterdam and printed a map, and now headed in what she hoped was the right direction.

Funny, she'd expected less foot traffic, given that the residents of Georgia had been through a war not so long ago. Instead, street cafés and vendors selling ice cream and hot dogs festooned the sidewalks. Strollers scattered pigeons, and the occasional artist called out a price.

Normalcy. A country in crisis craved it, perhaps.

She understood. Whenever she'd come home from a mission, especially a rescue, she'd dive into her routine—yoga, health food, Bible study on base and weekly phone calls home.

She hadn't had a real routine since she'd left the military. Which was why, perhaps, she was always living in crisis mode, pushing herself, never finding her default rhythm.

In a way, the foreign aromas made her feel more at home than anything had in the two years she'd spent in Seattle.

She turned onto George Balanchine Street and spotted the embassy set off from the road, wire fencing cordoning off Little America from the rest of the world. A guard station flanked a gate at the end of the rectangular fencing. A driveway beyond led to an enormous white building—austere in relation to the rich architecture of the Tbilisi streetscape. Of course, Americans had to be different, stand apart, resist blending in.

She hoped, however, just this once, her nephew hadn't listened to her advice and had done exactly that—*not* blended in. It would be a thousand times easier to find him if he'd left a conspicuous trail.

And as for this runaway girl…well, Mae hoped she was worth it.

The light changed and she stepped out to cross.

Something grabbed at the canvas bag slung across her body, jerking her back.

On instinct, she whirled around to slam her fist on the hand holding her bag. Didn't even think when she followed with a side kick to the shins.

She finished with a stiff arm chop to the neck.

The pickpocket didn't run. Didn't, in fact, even flinch. He just blocked her chop, his grip iron on her bag, dark eyes on hers, his voice just above a growl. "Calm down and stop hitting me."

Then he released her bag. Mae tripped back, words stuck in her throat.

Chet?

He looked good, too. Dark curly hair, a little shorter than she remembered. Rumpled in a gray snap-button denim shirt rolled up just above the elbows. And a messenger bag slung across his chest. He stared at her with those piercing blue eyes that seemed to be able, in this moment, to stun her into silence. Chet Stryker. The man who'd told her that she couldn't ever be on his team. That she couldn't keep up.

That he didn't want her in his life.

He had her off balance—that was why she let him drag her back toward the shadowy enclave between two doors. She was still reeling when he pushed her against the wall, bracketed her between his arms, and said tightly, "Can't you listen to anything I say?"

And then, because it felt right, because he deserved it, because all her adrenaline suddenly peaked, she hit him again.

Square in the chest. "Apparently not."

THREE

"Why do you always have to make things so difficult?" Chet rubbed his chest where Mae had boxed him. The first two punches he'd taken—after all, he had pounced on her like a bandit, but he'd been trying to keep her from igniting an international incident. The last thing he needed was to alert the local militia to his presence in the country.

The third punch, however, hurt more than it should have. Especially since Mae had looked him square in the face, full recognition in those beautiful green eyes, right before she walloped him.

Although he probably deserved that one, too. Not just for stomping on her hopes of flying for Stryker International, but also for walking out of her life.

Or perhaps for letting her believe that he could make room for her in his heart.

Okay, she still took up way too much room in his heart, but she didn't have to know that. No, that wouldn't be safe for anyone.

Mae stalked down the street, ten feet ahead of him, fists tight, as if she might be trying not to hit him again. He'd vote for that. In fact, he should probably be ecstatic that she was heading in the opposite direction of the embassy, that she'd bought his reasoning that the government would only send them packing stateside. Unfortunately, he'd expected—no, hoped was more accurate—that she'd actually be happy to see him. That her eyes would light up, and maybe she'd throw her arms around him.

He'd been jostled around the cargo hold of the C-130 harder than he'd thought.

She looked better than the image his imagination had conjured up. Her auburn hair had grown, and she wore it in a sloppy, curly, tantalizing ponytail. Despite trying to hide her figure inside a pair of baggy cargo pants, a green T-shirt and a canvas jacket, she took his breath away. She still looked like she had the day he'd met her—about ready to bullet a group of disrespectful teenage boys with gooey tortilla wraps.

They'd deserved it. He would have helped her, even. Something about her—the spark in her eye, the pride in her jaw, the way she turned away, hiding her pain—stirred his respect. Of course, he knew the story—thanks to his pal David Curtiss, one of Mae's college buddies—of how she'd risked her life for her friend Roman and rescued him from a Siberian gulag, and just what it had netted her.

No pension. No job. Stripped of her very identity as a soldier.

Seeing her pain had made him suddenly long to make it all better. To make her smile.

Just another person he'd managed to disappoint.

At least he hadn't gotten her killed.

Yet.

Unfortunately, it might be easier to reason with a rhinoceros than with Mae when she was in this kind of mood.

He dashed to catch up and was on her heel when she whirled. He plowed right into her and had to grab her to keep them both from going over.

She shook out of his grip. Opened her mouth. Closed it. Glared him into a pile of ash.

"Still not using our words, are we?" Chet stepped back and held up his hands. "Okay, I'll fill in the blanks. I'm here to help you find your nephew. And the runaway princess."

For the first time, her expression flickered. He leaped on it.

"Yep, I said princess. From a Caucasian tribe. Did you know she's pledged to be married in a few days, and guess who ran off with the bride?"

Mae's expression drained and she rolled her

eyes—or perhaps looked heavenward for help. Which he was all for, at the moment.

"The bottom line is, your nephew is in big trouble, and I'm here to find him." He reached into his jacket and pulled out a plane ticket. "Alone. You're headed back to the states, Mae."

Before you get killed.

"In your wildest dreams, pal." Mae turned on her heel.

Well, uh, yes, actually. Because in his *nightmares* she stuck around to get tortured and killed by Akif Bashim.

He grabbed her wrist. "I'll drag you to the airport if I have to."

She snapped her wrist away. "I never thought I'd actually be glad to say this, but…you're not my boss."

He flinched a little at that. "No, but I do know this country and what happens when people get caught in the crossfire. Which, if you didn't happen to notice, is exactly what's happening in that little hot spot of the world Josh and his girlfriend seem to have gone walkabout in. So, yes, honey, you're leaving."

Mae, as if deaf, kept walking.

"Oh, nice, Mae."

She ignored him. And where exactly was she going? He sped up behind her, matching her long strides. "I thought you might be glad to see me— after all, *you* called *me*."

She stomped along in silence.

"C'mon, Mae, listen to me. I am on your side here, believe it or not. It'll be better for Josh if you go and let me track him down. I can travel faster, and I know the language and—"

She stopped.

He skidded to a halt and took a step back. "What?"

Her stare could probably leave blisters. "You want me to leave so I won't get in the way, is that it? It's too *risky* to work with me, so you'll just kick me to the curb?"

He opened his mouth, ready to refute her, but of course nothing came out. Because, as usual, she'd bulls-eyed it. He lifted a shoulder in a rueful shrug.

She shook her head, as if dispelling some inner voice, and stared at him a long time. *Oh, Mae, why do you make this all so hard?* Why couldn't she be the kind of woman who didn't have to be on the front lines of trouble? The one who'd let him take her out for ice cream? The girl he'd envisioned on the other end of his emails? The one he'd known for a crazy, romantic week in Seattle?

Or maybe he hadn't known her at all.

She finally spoke, her words losing some of their

heat, yet still stiff with anger. "If you knew anything about me, anything at all, Chet, you would know that I will not just go home and leave Josh here. I'm not built that way. I don't know what's going on with him—why he did this, or who this *princess* is—" She added air quotes, as if he couldn't catch her tone.

"She's the daughter of a warlord."

"Perfect. For all I know, he's being held against his will. But I made a promise to my sister. And I keep my promises."

Right. He did know that about her.

"So, you go ahead and do whatever you need to do. Find the princess, save the world. Whatever. But you need to stay out of *my* way. *Yasna?*"

He hated it when she spoke Russian. It only reminded him that she had friends and experiences that didn't fit into the neat, safe world he wanted her to live in. Worse, as she met his eyes, unblinking, he saw that the anger had vanished, only to be replaced by something more frightening.

Resolve.

And when she turned and stalked out again for parts unknown, all he could do was follow.

Wasn't this just swell? He had four days to find a runaway princess, talk her into helping save the world by marrying a man twice her age, and stop a love-struck teenager from starting an international incident, all while trying to keep up with—forget ahead of—the woman he most wanted to protect in the world.

He'd felt more comfortable in his Snow White costume.

"Just tell me where you're—*we're*—going, please."

"The market," she said without looking at him.

The market. Okay. He cataloged the changes in Tbilisi as he followed her down the street. The smell—dust, car exhaust, the slightest whiff of grilled lamb—all seemed familiar. He didn't recognize, however, the red and blue vendor kiosks selling ice cream and candy, the electric beat of European bands banging from boom boxes. Traffic hummed and horns blared, motors coughing out black smoke from Russian-made vehicles—*Ladas* and *Zhigulis,* he supposed—but also Japanese imports and even German Volkswagens. It all evidenced a new capitalism, not the Georgia he'd remembered.

Of course, when he'd been sneaking around Georgia, it had been in the hills, back when the Russians occupied the offices in the ornate buildings in downtown Tbilisi, back when his government decided that a little revolutionary thinking might help take down communism. His stomach churned as he pondered the fact that the seeds he'd sown over two decades ago still wreaked havoc in the country today. Back then, he'd believed he was arming freedom. Oh, hindsight.

A woman, her head covered, holding her toddler daughter in her lap as she sat on the grimy sidewalk, held out a hand to him as he passed by. He couldn't meet her eyes as he dropped a *lari* into her grip. Just ten feet away, yet another woman, this one much younger, huddled under her veils in the alcove of a Soviet-era building peering at him with huge brown eyes.

Carissa.

He inhaled so sharply that Mae glanced at him.

Of course it wasn't Carissa. Couldn't be. But memory had sharp claws and it knew how to make him bleed.

If not cost him his life, this time around.

Maybe he should have called Wick and the rest of Stryker International instead of packing his duffel and hopping on a transport without so much as a check-in. His team would show up at the office and read the hastily scrawled, "Off on a private trip. Be back soon." And since he hadn't taken a day off since he'd started Stryker International, those cryptic words would have the opposite of the intended effect, igniting speculation, if not an all-out manhunt. Starting with a phone call to his partner, Vicktor Shubnikov.

With some more rotten luck, Vicktor would mention it to his wife, Gracie, who would immediately think of her former roomie, Mae, and probably follow up with a phone call to Seattle. To which she'd get no answer.

How long, really, would it take his team to figure out he'd headed to Georgia, scrounge up a plane and stir an already-simmering mess to full boil?

Clearly, Chet had needed more coffee and a few moments to think before running off after trouble.

Trouble who seemed to be outdistancing him despite his near run. Sheesh, Mae had long legs.

"Slow down."

"Keep up."

She cut through the crowd and down the stairs of a metro entrance. He nearly tripped over yet another woman wrapped in a blanket selling walnuts, then followed Mae through the glass doors into the station. Political posters or advertisements for upcoming events, concerts and theater productions, even an ad for cigarettes papered the walls, their tattered edges ruffling against the rush of outside air. The subway rumbled beneath their feet, its hum muted.

She stopped, just for a moment, reading a sign, then consulted a map she had wadded in her hand.

"The market is located on—"

"I know where it is," she snapped.

Good grief. He brushed past her, headed toward the red line.

He heard her following and smiled.

She said nothing as they took the escalator down, boarded the metro and rode it to their stop. He recognized it now—the smells, the familiar fatigued, gray-eyed expressions of the passengers, the rattle of the metro as it snaked beneath the crust of Tbilisi. He'd met Carissa on a subway, had planned it that way—a "chance" meeting. Remembering made him tighten his grip on the steel overhead bar. Mae looked out the window, away from him.

He couldn't remember how much of his past he'd shared with Mae. Enough, clearly, for her to know he had contacts here. Maybe not enough to tell her how much he regretted them.

At the time, email had seemed a much safer way to reveal his heart without giving too much of it away.

He startled when a hand gripped his arm. Mae gazed up at him, a strange look in her eyes. Something not unlike…pity?

"Nothing is going to happen to me. We'll get Josh and get out. It'll be fine, I promise."

So maybe he had told her—at least parts of it.

But he couldn't reply. Because he knew better than anyone that it was a promise she couldn't keep.

It was something about the look in his eyes, the way he gripped the overhead bar, his knuckles nearly white. The way he'd gasped seeing the homeless woman. Being back in Georgia seemed to cause Chet actual pain.

Mae let his arm go, but the answer to the question she'd asked him so long ago now flashed in his eyes.

"Have you ever lost someone you cared about?"

The question probably had come too quickly for both of them, but his leave had flown by and he'd been heading back to D.C. within days. They'd crammed everything they could into one short week of vacation. It had felt like a wartime romance, and she'd begun to fall for the man. Or at least, what she knew of him. He tuned his rental car radio to classical, he *used* the hotel gym, he opened car doors and bought her dinner and rescued her from the mess her life had become. With Chet she didn't feel like a failure, the one left standing alone with the broken pieces. Chet made her see possibility. Made her feel…worthwhile.

Valuable.

A shadow had crossed his face when she'd asked the question, even in the late-afternoon dimness of the coffee shop as the rain poured down upon Seattle. A shadow that had tightened her stomach as his hand reached for the platinum chain around his neck.

"Yes. Once, a small lifetime ago. She died. I was on a mission, and she got caught in the crossfire." He said it while staring into his macchiato, turning the cup quietly.

She let a tick of time pass, waiting for more until finally she just covered his hand with hers.

She put the rest together later, over time, reading between the lines of his letters. He'd been working undercover in Georgia while it was still under Russian influence, before the civil war between Ossetia and Georgia. He'd been captured, his men had to rescue him, there'd been casualties. From David, she'd learned that Chet blamed himself.

Seeing him now in the subway, steeling himself against what could only be a flood of memories, still wearing that mysterious chain, her frustration drained. *Of course* he wanted to send her home. He feared the worst. He had to—it was built into him.

Chet looked down at her, as if measuring her words.

Then he took her hand and enclosed it in his own.

So maybe he did miss her, just a little.

Mae still couldn't believe he'd come all the way to Tbilisi. She hated the feelings that knowledge sparked, the thrill that had her heart thrumming in overdrive.

Perhaps she shouldn't have hit him...that *last* time.

The subway stopped and he released her hand. "This is us."

She followed the crowd off the subway, a tight clutch on her bag. A real pickpocket would have a heyday with the American dollars she'd kept unchanged to use in barter.

"Let's see if we can track down some transportation," she said as they emerged a block away from the market.

"Please tell me that food is included in your agenda," Chet said. She glanced at him—he did look a little pale.

"We'll grab a *shashlik* on the way."

"You're worse than David."

She smiled at that. David, Chet's undercover teammate back when they both served Uncle Sam, had a reputation for job first, food and fun second. Although hanging out with him at Moscow University could easily be counted one of the happiest times in her life.

"Hey, he's my hero, so don't be dissin' him."

"He's my hero, too. Just has a problem with the fact that the humans around him have to eat," Chet said, touching her elbow as they entered the market.

The odor of grilled meats, rotting fruits, truck exhaust and garbage spiced the air. Rock music pulsed from ancient bookshelf speakers bracketing kiosks selling pirated CDs; between the beats rose the noise of horns, dogs barking, customers bartering.

Vendors, Caucasian men wearing dark pants and leather jackets or wool-wrapped babushkas, perched behind stacks of potatoes or apples, bins of walnuts, and trays of *hochapuri,* and haggled with customers, making change out of black fanny packs. They passed a group of men, hunched on the ground, watching passersby and drinking dark Turkish beer.

Mae kept her bag in front of her, wrapping an arm around it.

She stopped in front of a vendor wiping vegetable oil on a skewer of char-darkened lamb. "Two, please," she said in Russian, holding out a *lari.*

The man wiped his hands on his crusty apron, grabbed a towel and wrapped it around one end of the cheap aluminum skewer. He handed her one and Chet the other.

Mae took her skewer. "Now you aren't the only one who has ever bought lunch."

Chet pried one of the meat chunks off the skewer. "I like buying lunch. But thanks."

They threaded their way past piles of unnamed red meat, whole chickens with their legs poking into the air, plastic bags filled with flour or kasha, burlap sacks of rice, piles of fresh herbs, garlic, radishes, carrots and rutabagas. She didn't meet the eyes of the numerous leather-coated men standing sentry, smoking away their days as market mafia.

Chet kept his mouth shut as he walked behind her, his profile low.

She located the trucks in the back of the market, their tailgates open as the men from the outlying villages sold fresh eggs and dairy products—milk and creamy white chunks of cheese.

She studied her choices—rounded older men with teeth rotted from black chew, younger guys, wearing the black garb of their urban peers. One teen, however, stood out to her, a boy of about seventeen, wearing a ratty brown sweater and fraying tennis shoes splattered with mud. He unloaded eggs from the back of a green pickup, the sides shuttered with rickety fencing.

He greeted her with wary dark eyes as she approached.

"Dobri deen," she said softly, the Russian for "good afternoon" rolling off her tongue easily. Although the official language was Georgian now, fifteen years ago, under Communist rule, the schools all taught Russian.

Beside her, Chet scanned the other merchants like a Doberman.

The boy nodded his response.

"We're looking for a ride to Burmansk. Are you going there?"

He regarded her for a moment, then hopped down from his truck. His eyes darted beyond her, then back again. "Maybe."

"Maybe" was always a good answer. She lowered her voice. "I have dollars. And we need to leave soon."

Chet tensed beside her. She heard his slow intake of breath. She didn't move, keeping her gaze on the boy. He tightened his lips, darted another look around, then nodded. "I have to finish unloading."

"We'll get supplies and meet back here in an hour," Chet said, sounding nearly native with half-Arabic, half-Slavic tones.

The boy looked at him with surprise, as if he'd just materialized there. Fear ringed his eyes.

So maybe Chet would come in handy, just in case a village boy considered ulterior motives.

They scoured the market for food, blankets and equipment. Chet turned all business, bartering prices down, adding to their supplies things she hadn't considered—matches, cups, rain ponchos, a medical kit.

"Are we going camping?"

"You never know what's out there, and what we might find," Chet said as he added a can of sardines to his pack.

She dearly hoped it would be Josh and his new girlfriend.

And that, no matter what they found, she wouldn't be losing her heart along the way.

FOUR

"Mae, wake up. Wake up."

"I'm awake." She hadn't been until the last nudge, when the strident, panicked tone in Chet's whisper sliced through her dreams.

She'd been reliving their goodbye on her apartment balcony overlooking the sound, the air crisp and heady with fall, Chet's strong arms around her. How had she fallen so totally for this man in the space of a week? She felt as if she'd known him nearly all her life—knew his smile, knew the look in his eyes that made her feel like the only woman in the room. In the universe. And finally, *finally,* the night before he would leave—for who knew where or how long, thank you, Uncle Sam—he decided to pull her to him, wrap those muscular arms around her waist, curve one hand behind her neck to draw her face—

"We're at a checkpoint," Chet said, his lips close to her ear. Because, of course, as if her heart had a homing beacon, in her sleep she'd curled up and pillowed her head on his chest. Good grief. She went to push away, but he held her, his arms tightening. "Don't move."

She remembered climbing into the truck—the back of course, because Chet wasn't about to get trapped in the cab, or worse, be banished to the back while she squished in between the teenager and his overweight, leering uncle who had joined them for the trip home.

Chet had instead made a comfy travel compartment for them between two stacks of wooden boxes, atop a folded blanket just large enough for them to sit on with their legs drawn up. To shield them from view, he'd pulled over them a red and white tarp he'd found wadded up in the back.

Under which, she'd fallen soundly asleep. And Chet played right along, apparently, stretching out his legs to cradle her in his embrace. She tried to whisk his smell—masculine, strong—from her thoughts.

"Who are they?"

"Russian soldiers, from the sound of it. They're patrolling the area south of Ossetia. It's officially Georgian country, but they are the so-called peacekeepers."

She listened to the voices, one of them demanding passports from the teen and his uncle. "Peacemakers?"

"AKA thugs. Shh."

Okay. She slowed her breathing and tuned her ears, but she'd heard only the churn of Chet's heartbeat as he held her tight. If she didn't know better, she'd think he might be sca—

"What's in the back?"

Footsteps.

Chet reached behind him and his hand emerged with a gun. *A gun?* Clearly someone had expected more than a camping trip. She looked up and met his eyes. He shook his head ever so slightly.

"Nothing. Egg cartons. Boxes. Check for yourself."

Chet drew a breath. Mae froze. *Please, God, please, please. Oh, why did I get Chet into this—*

The boxes moved, the tarp rustled. A horn blared from behind them.

"Nichevo zdes."

Yes, nothing here. Mae closed her eyes. *Nothing here.*

Beside her, Chet's breath leaked out.

The truck lurched forward, spilling out exhaust.

Chet safetied his gun and tucked it back behind him.

Mae tried to push away from him, but his arms locked around her. "Just a minute longer."

They must have turned off the main drag onto something gravel because the truck lurched, the wooden side rails chattering like teeth as they rumbled down the road.

Finally, his arms loosened and he helped her sit up.

She finger-combed her hair and fished around in her pocket for a breath mint. "How long was I out?"

"Less than an hour. But long enough. Look for yourself." He edged the tarp back to reveal the terrain.

She didn't know what to do with the chokehold of emotions. Where there had been rolling countryside dotted now and again with blue, yellow and green houses, great trenches furrowed the land, uprooting it in ugly channels filled with mangled trees and the charred carcasses of tanks, rocket launchers and jeeps. Fences lay in splinters and fire-blackened windows mourned, peering across the land from houses with imploded roofs or walls reduced to rubble.

Beyond that lay the jagged cityscape, the closest apartments raked raw, as if a great hand had clawed down their faces, exposing the insides to the world. Curtains fluttered in the wind, and a bed and mattress falling out of a gaping hole, seemed as if they might be leaping to safety.

The inhabitants surely hadn't found safety.

Mae pressed against her stomach, unsure if the roiling meant horror or hunger.

"They were already poor, struggling people, just finding their feet after the last civil war." Chet lowered the tarp. "What was your nephew doing here?"

"Humanitarian aid for a local mission with a group from college. He came for a month this summer. The others returned about a week ago, in time for classes—we don't know why he stayed."

"Love can do that to you—make you forget your priorities."

Mae glanced at him. "Maybe his priorities changed."

"Yeah, so much that he was willing to risk another civil war. Or worse."

"Or worse?"

She flinched at his sharp look. "Do you understand the stakes here, Mae?"

"Yes, I understand the stakes." Good grief, she wasn't naïve. She'd been in the military herself, if he cared to remember. "Josh fell in love with the wrong girl. Apparently, she didn't tell him that she was some tribal princess, or he never would have jeopardized 'international peace.'" She bracketed the words with her fingers. "I assure you that once we find him, we'll explain to him that he needs to set things right with her family and everything will work out."

"Are you kidding me? Do you have any idea who this 'princess' is?" Chet mimicked her gesture, clearly to mock her. "She's the daughter of one of the CIA's top ten terrorists. And she's agreed to marry in order to keep the world from plunging into World War Three. If your nephew doesn't accidentally start it first."

"What are you talking about?"

"I'm talking about the CIA. Your nephew's girlfriend works for them, and she's just reneged on a deal to go covert for them in Iran. So, unless we track them down and convince her to marry her betrothed, the world will be a much more dangerous place. Not to mention that Akif will probably blame the U.S., and by proxy, Georgia, for the loss of his bride price. Which means that he'll figure out a way to break the cease-fire. Probably with more bombs. And that's just one of the many scenarios that could happen here. So, yes, I think your nephew has completely lost sight of his priorities, sweetheart."

She didn't know where to start—with the "sweetheart" or the glaring, abrupt fact that he *hadn't* come here to help her, at least not in the way she'd thought. Clearly, he'd been sent here on his *own* mission, maybe even by the CIA—a truth she felt like a backhand to her heart. A mission that had about nil to do with her, and everything to do with forcing some girl to marry against her will.

Somewhere in the back of her consciousness, she was picking up the bleeding remains of her too-easily wooed heart, but in the forefront, all she could see was the brutal truth.

Chet Stryker was exactly the male chauvinist jerk she'd pegged him to be—a guy who decided a woman couldn't fly airplanes for him, who didn't allow women choices, making their decisions for them.

Like the kind of career they could have.

Or the men they should marry.

She should be glad she'd gotten away from him when she did.

She retreated as far as she could from him, drawing up her knees, holding them against herself. "I'll tell you right now, Josh's priorities are the same as mine. Save the girl from letches like you."

He flinched but said nothing as they jolted down the road.

She buried her head in her arms, hating that she'd let herself—for even one second—think he'd come here for her, that he might have changed, that he respected her, believed in her.

Loved her.

Maybe *she* had lost sight of *her* priorities.

The truck hit a pothole, banged them hard against the metal surface, and then, with an ear-splitting squeal, lurched to a stop. As Mae lifted her head, the truck gave a final shudder, burped its last and died.

"End of the road," Chet said quietly as he listened to the boy and his uncle mutter over the engine. "And the longer we sit here, the worse the odds of us picking up another ride." He peered again from under the tarp. The sun bled through the jagged mountainscape of the northern Caucasus to the west, casting bruised shadows into the valley and gullies and over the broken city of Gori, now to their south. Their ride must have turned onto a side road, a shortcut, perhaps, off the main Georgian highway, now under reconstruction.

"How far are we from Burmansk?" Mae asked, her tone glacial. Yeah, this trip had turned extra-fun since he'd offered up a dose of reality. But maybe Mae Lund needed to pull her head out of fairy-tale land and start realizing that her actions had consequences. And in this case, the potential consequences involved war—possibly a world war at that.

"By truck? Maybe an hour. By foot?" He lifted a shoulder. "I hope you brought your hiking shoes." He reached out his hand to help her up. She ignored it and found her feet on her own, stretching.

Fine. No one asked her to like him. Probably it was better this way. Letch, huh? Well, maybe. He felt like one a little, hating the facts.

Yes, he was going to bring Miss Runaway back to her village.

To be sold into marital slavery, CIA deal notwithstanding.

In order to save lives.

Just when was one life worth more than many?

He couldn't let himself ponder that as he hopped out of the truck. Instead, he focused on the fact that Mae believed he was exactly what she'd called him. A letch. A man who used women. Clearly she'd forgotten his emails to her, written during his years working undercover, fighting human trafficking on the other side of the world. They detailed how it chewed him up to see women abused. And later, how he'd nearly given his life to help David take down the trafficking ring. Words of pain filled those emails, churned out from the horrors he'd seen.

Maybe that was all they were. Words. She'd never really seen the man he was, or wanted to be.

He hadn't either, actually. Not for a long time, at least.

Now he saw the truth in her demeanor as she

stalked away from him on the dirt road. She despised him.

Frankly, that hurt more than his aching muscles or the fatigue weighting his bones. Because, for approximately forty minutes, as she'd slept in his arms, he let himself believe that maybe they could put things right, and find their friendship again. That maybe he could connect with someone who knew him, understood him.

Or at least understood the Chet he'd edited into the man she wanted.

"Spaceeba," Mae said to the teenager, and handed him a wad of dollars. Chet kept his eyes on the uncle, who'd edged toward her, as if he might decide to up the fee.

He moved next to his nephew, spitting on the ground, his doughy stomach swelling from his button shirt. *"Zhenshina!"*

Mae turned, and Chet took a step toward them. Wonderful. Apparently, the old man wasn't quite done with them. Which meant that Chet would have to step in. He saw an ugly scenario materializing before his eyes, one where he'd have to stop the old man and his nephew from alerting the authorities to their presence. In front of Mae, no less.

So she could add "brute" to her list of identities.

"Eta carta." The man extended to her a grimy pack of paper.

A map?

Mae took it, opened it. "It's a map of the region. He's marked Burmansk."

Oh. Apparently he'd jumped to conclusions.

Mae held out her hand. *"Spaceeba."*

The old man took it, leaning in to kiss her cheek. She let him as Chet cataloged his every movement, just in case he might be emptying out her bag while he did it.

"C Bogom," the uncle said, drawing away.

Go with God. Well, a guy couldn't be too careful.

The glittering lights of the city behind them beckoned, tiny stars luring them in the wrong direction. Chet briefly considered turning back, slipping into the city under darkness, maybe boosting a car. But with Russian brown boys armed, restless and roaming, and Mae ready to bolt, hoofin' it west into the dark beyond seemed the best option.

"Ready?" he asked Mae, who had flicked on her penlight and was studying the map.

She stared at the stars as if orienting herself. Of course, being a pilot, she would know the sky. Then she set off. No words, not a backward glance to say, *Hey, you coming?* Just off she went, over the embankment, into the brush.

With him scampering after her.

He could barely make out her outline against the velvety night, but the wind mercifully picked up her scent and twined it back to him. He followed the scuff of her boots on the grass and quickly caught up.

"Don't wait for me or anything."

"I told you—keep up."

He clenched his jaw, wanting to hit something, hard. Like maybe himself, for losing his temper with her in the truck. Or for thinking that she might still care about him. Clearly, his heart hadn't quite scabbed over.

They walked in silence as the night canopied them, the stars winking above, spectators to his misery. The wind turned brisk, curling down from the far mountains, and after a while, she pulled a blanket from her pack and wrapped it around her like a Bedouin.

But she kept walking—the energizer bunny—whereas he could probably flop down next to a boulder and sleep for the next year. He rubbed his hands, sticking them again into his pockets.

"Are you still flying?"

She said nothing, and he began to wonder if she were ever going to acknowledge his presence again when she said, "Of course. I could no more stop flying than stop breathing. Except that sometimes I want to, given the fact I'm flying tourists who occasionally barf on me. Thanks for asking."

She didn't look at him when she spoke, and he couldn't tell if she were kidding.

"They barf on you?"

"That's what happens when people don't follow the rules. Someone gets the brunt of it."

He had the feeling that maybe she wasn't referring only to her passengers. But what rules had he broken?

"How's your sister—Josh's mom, right?"

"You remember I have a sister? Wow. I am impressed."

"Hey, I remember everything you ever wrote to me," he said. "You're the one with the selective amnesia."

She whirled, pointing a finger dangerously close to his face. It shook. He waited. Then she put it down, breathing out deeply. "I remember, too."

In the moonlight, her eyes glistened. Then she turned away. "Even if I wish I didn't."

He watched her go for a moment.

Oh.

He followed without a word, measuring the sounds of the night, animals scampering through the grass, the wind in the trees. Smoke, from a fire somewhere, tinged the air.

"How's your business?" Her voice emerged flat and stone tired as it came out of the darkness. She could be talking to keep herself awake.

Terrible. I don't have a clue what I'm doing. I need you, and not just to fly. "Fine."

"How's Vicktor?"

Over-the-moon in love with his wife, who worries about her former roommate, and doesn't leave well enough alone every time I have dinner with them. She can't understand why I don't hire you, either. "He's good. So's Gracie."

"She writes me. And calls occasionally. So, I know."

You know? Do you know that I told Vicktor that I made a mistake? That I panicked and pushed the one good thing out of my life? "That's nice."

She stopped talking.

It was when she stumbled that he decided on a change of leadership. "We need some rest, Mae. We won't be able to find anything in the dark."

"I'm not tired."

"Well, I am." So far they'd avoided the forests, but now he hooked her hand and pulled her toward a swath of trees, using his flashlight to locate shelter next to a downed oak. He pulled out the poncho, spreading it out in the cleft of the branches, then he sat and pulled the blanket over him. On top of that, he draped the second poncho for rain protection. He held up one side. "I know you don't like me much, but it'll be warmer if we stick together." He patted the ground next to him, trying to keep it casual, hoping, somewhere in the back of his mind, that she might fall asleep again in his arms. Even if by accident.

She seemed to contemplate her options.

"I promise not to be a letch."

His joke fell flat. Still, she sat down next to him and let him put the poncho over her. "What if someone finds us?"

"We're in the middle of the woods—"

She flashed her light against the folds of the forest. "What was that about trigger-happy Russian soldiers?"

"Okay, fine. I'm sleeping. You stand watch. Wake me in four hours. Then I'll take a shift."

He curled into a ball and tucked the blanket tighter around himself. Hopefully by tomorrow she'd be out of his life, his misery over. Hallelujah.

She stared out into the darkness, probably thinking the same thing.

Dear Chet,
I know you must be out of touch right now—you haven't answered my previous two emails—

but I've decided to just keep writing, and when you get this you'll know that someone cares. I spent Thanksgiving weekend with my sister and her son, Josh. He's a senior in high school—I can hardly believe it. It seems like only yesterday he was just learning to walk, navigating from our old green sofa to the Formica table to the back bedroom which he shared with my sister.

I'm going to miss him. In a way, he's like my own son—before I went into the army, mine was the only consistent face he saw. My sister spent the first three years of his life trying to finish high school, and occasionally disappearing for long weekends, trying to forget that she became a mother at thirteen. My leaving for the army forced her to grow up, maybe, although it didn't help my mother, who still hasn't figured out that she doesn't need any of the deadbeats she brings home. Thankfully, she stopped letting them move in about the time I turned twelve and her sodden boyfriend turned his attentions toward me.

I probably shouldn't have told you all that, but I felt it was only fair to tell you that I don't come from the stellar West Point family you do. You should have all the facts.

I don't suppose you managed a morsel of

turkey or cranberry dressing over the weekend? I miss you, and am praying for you. Stay
safe.
Yours,
Mae

Yours. The word pulsed in his head, the memory
of receiving her email fresh as if it had been yesterday. He hadn't had a Thanksgiving turkey—in
fact, he'd spent the weekend holed up in surveillance, watching a Chinese mobster beat the stuffin'
out of a fellow agent, helpless to intervene. He'd
crawled back to his flat feeling raw and alone, only
to discover her emails.

I am praying for you. Stay safe.

He outlined her now against the darkness, seeing
her as a teenager, trying to keep her mother sober,
her sister safe, her nephew in clean diapers, and
food on the table. And yes, when he'd read the
letter, an ugly part of him wanted to track down
her mother's perverted boyfriend and take out his
eyes, and maybe some other parts.

But most of all, he couldn't get past the fact
that she'd trusted him with the broken parts of
herself...

She had deserved more from him.

At the very least, with a rush of clarity, he understood why she'd trek halfway across the world after her lost nephew. He could barely remember his own nephew's name—or maybe he had two of them. He hadn't talked to his sister for a number of years now, since the death of the General. His mother lived in a retirement community in Florida, he knew that much from the direct deposit address on his bank stubs.

But if any of them vanished in a foreign country? Well, he might find out on the news, or perhaps through one of his father's old chums. But drop everything, his career, even his life?

No, he hadn't deserved a friend like Mae. As she sat in the darkness, a silhouette of resolve, he knew that much.

He should have given back to her at least what she'd given him.

Trust.

FIVE

You're the one with the selective amnesia.

She wiped her cheek with the back of her hand, watching Chet in the dappled moonlight. He'd dropped off to sleep in roughly a millisecond.

She didn't have a prayer of sleeping. Not with his words ricocheting through her head.

Selective amnesia?

Hardly.

She had his letters practically memorized— every lying, deceitful word. *I was hoping we could build a life...* She'd looked it up when she returned from Moscow, after Gracie's wedding empty-handed, her future like a wind sock on a lifeless day, limp and dead. Yes, he'd written that. Twice, in fact.

The first time he'd written that, she'd attributed his words to heavy pain meds. After all, that particular letter had arrived shortly after David Curtiss had, under duress and to keep his cover, put a gun to Chet and shot him clear through his gut. But he'd written those words again after he'd emerged from deep cover.

When he decided to move to Prague.

So, what exactly had happened?

Priorities. His own company, on his terms. She'd realized right after he'd told her she couldn't be on his team that she probably didn't know him at all.

And he'd proven that with his announcement in the truck. He wasn't here for Josh or her. He wanted to save the world, be some sort of international hero, whatever it took and whoever he ran over.

She leaned back against the trunk, her eyes to the heavens. Why, Lord, was it so hard for her to let go of this man? Clearly he wasn't the person she'd fallen for in Seattle, or even the man she'd met in his letters.

Folding her hands, she shivered as the night closed in around them. If only the spongy forest floor didn't offer such a compelling enticement to curl up in the loam and let fatigue wash over her. She exhaled a long breath...

"Stop! No!"

Mae jerked awake.

"No!" Beside her, Chet thrashed against his dreams.

Shoot. After all her bravado, she'd fallen asleep.

The sky had just begun to wax gray, blotting out the stars, dawn just below the horizon.

He cried out again and she pressed her hand to his chest. "Chet, wake up."

Something had a hold on him, something violent and agonizing, and it shook him underneath his blanket.

"Chet!"

He woke with a start, blue eyes wide, looking at her but not seeing.

"It's me, Mae. You were having a nightmare."

He shuddered out a breath. He still didn't seem to see her.

"Chet." She ran her hand down his face, over the stubble of whiskers. "Wake up."

He curled his fingers around her wrist, turning his face into her hand.

She froze. "Chet, wake up."

Perhaps her tone, rich with shock, and too much longing, brought him to himself. He blinked, and then his eyes found hers. "Mae?"

"You had a nightmare." She gently pulled her wrist from his grasp, hoping he didn't remember that part.

He sat up, the blanket fell, and he shook, running his hands down his face.

Oh, Chet. He fought wars even in his sleep. He

lifted his face, and even in the wan light she made out fatigue, a press of sorrow in his eyes.

"Do you want to talk about it?" she asked softly.

He didn't look at her. "Is it my watch?"

Okay, so they *weren't* going to talk about the demon that had him thrashing about, screaming in the leaves. His words swept fatigued tears into her eyes.

"I think it's time to go. It's almost light out, and we probably need to figure out where we are."

He stared at her. "But what about you? You need sleep."

"I'm fine."

"Why didn't you wake me?"

"I— Oh, *fine*. I fell asleep, too. For a little while."

A smile, not unkind, edged up his face. "I'll pretend you didn't tell me that."

"That works for me."

He wiped his forehead with his sleeve, sweaty despite the fact their breath puffed in the early morning air. And of course, while she probably had makeup smudged under her eyes—whatever remained of it—and smelled like a gopher, he looked devastating with his two-day shadow and forever-mussed dark hair. He even smelled good— woodsy, with a hint of masculine muskiness.

She had to give him props for managing to find them a stellar hiding place, especially in the dead of night. He'd tucked them behind a fallen oak with webbed roots that sheltered their covey from the field just beyond. The murmuring of cattle stirred the morning air, carrying with it the earthy musk of a nearby farm.

Next to her, Chet plowed through his duffel bag. "How about something to eat?"

She glanced at him. "Are you sure you're okay? That seemed like a pretty vivid nightmare—"

"Found it." He produced a piece of halvah in gray paper.

Sesame seeds in a honey paste for breakfast. She decided to consider it Russian granola. "I used to love halvah in college," she said as she took the snack.

He chewed in silence beside her, clearly not wanting to discuss his nightmare. He finished the halvah, then pulled out an orange, peeled it and divided it with her.

"How many miles to Burmansk?" he finally asked.

The fruit splashed sweet and tangy in her mouth. She chased the breakfast with water and wiped her mouth with her grimy shirt. "I can't tell on this map—the legend is all off. I think maybe ten or fifteen, cross country?"

He took another bite. As he unscrewed his bottled water, she noticed his hands shaking.

She touched his forearm. "I'm sorry you got dragged into this, Chet."

He glanced at her, a sideways look. "I'm not. I would only be back in Prague, pacing the floor, worried sick about you."

He would? Her throat turned pasty. She took another sip of water. His eyes had fastened on her, as if reading her reaction.

"What?"

He got up, pulling out another orange from his bag. "Forget it. I shouldn't have said that." Crunching away through the leaves, he stood staring out into the field.

"I get it, you know. I realize what it cost you to come back here. I saw it in your eyes. You're remembering your mission, aren't you? The person you lost that you cared about. This—" she gestured to the forest and fields, to Georgia "—is bringing it all back."

He half turned to her, and she saw him wince, his jaw tight.

The cadence of the forest highlighted his silence.

"Sometimes I just feel like my mistakes could consume me whole."

He said it so softly that if she hadn't been staring

right at him, watching his lips, she wouldn't have heard it. But the mourning in his tone brought her to her feet.

By the time she reached him, he'd turned away from her again. "Her name was Carissa. She worked for a Georgian politician, and we were planning a coup. She could lay her hands on troop movements, get a hold of insider information we needed."

"We, meaning Americans?"

He winced. "Let's just say that sometimes Western governments give a little nudge to fledgling revolutionary groups for the sake of freedom."

She stayed silent.

"I was a soldier, following orders."

She gave a small nod when he glanced over his shoulder at her.

"This is one of the reasons I struck out on my own. The lines just got too blurry."

"And the costs too high?"

He swallowed. "Yes."

Yes. "So, what happened?"

A rush of sparrows scattered into the sky. He froze, listening. Then, quietly, "She got caught. Akif Bashim executed her."

Executed her. "Chet—" She put her hand on his arm. He didn't shrug it away. Neither, however, did he look at her. A bird chirruped down at them. The wind nudged the fallen leaves at their feet. "I'm so sorry."

He nodded.

Oh, Chet. She heard her words, resonating from a place inside even as she spoke them, just above a whisper. "Sometimes there's a wound inside so deep, it can steal your breath with its completeness. At times, it feels as fresh as the day you were injured. And you wonder in that moment if God has turned away from you, horrified at your ugliness, and if it is ever possible to be whole again."

Now, he looked at her, his eyes reddened. "How did you know that?"

"They're your words, Chet. You wrote them in a letter not long after you were shot. I remember wondering if they were about your injury, or something more."

He stared at his palm, rubbing his thumb over it. "Something more."

How she wanted to give him an answer, to tell him that yes, it was possible.

Yet she wasn't sure herself. Because sometimes just the intake of air over the shards of her mistakes could rake her over with pain. Sometimes she, too, wondered how God might put her together again.

If He even could.

"Did Bashim know you were involved?"

He kept rubbing his palm with his thumb. "Yeah. He was too busy beating me up to hear my team creep up on him. There was a gun battle, a few of his men were killed, and we hotfooted it out of the country."

Which meant he'd nearly been killed, too.

She didn't even bother to mask her horror as it trickled out in her taut voice. "And here you are again."

He inhaled, then raised his eyes to hers, and nodded.

"This must be a nightmare for you."

His jaw tightened.

Walking through this country probably felt like plowing through his own personal minefield. Mae's chest burned. "Why did you come back?"

His eyes caught hers, his voice so low it felt more like a breath whispered deep inside her chest. "You can't figure that out, Mae?"

And then just as she wanted to hurt him or hold him or do anything she could to calm the whir of panic inside, he reached out and wrapped his hand around her neck, pulled her to him, and kissed her.

It wasn't a gentle, tentative kiss, like it had been that night on the balcony, or even a sad kiss like the one he'd given her before he broke her heart in Moscow.

No, this kiss tasted of desperation and regret, of missing her, and needing her. His lips were sweet orange and spicy halvah, tasting of everything she'd remembered and more.

And for a second, she did nothing. Didn't move, didn't breathe. Just tried to get her bearings.

Then, it didn't matter. He wrapped his arms around her and she let herself kiss him with everything she wanted and everything she'd lost, forgetting how infuriating and bossy and overprotective and—

"I'm sorry." He broke away and brought his hand to cradle her jaw, his blue eyes in hers. "I'm so sorry."

Oh, no, not again…

She tried to move away but he held her, searching her eyes. "No, Mae, I'm not sorry for kissing you. I'm *sorry.* I'm sorry that I hurt you."

Oh. That sorry.

"And I'm sorry that I'm going to hurt you again."

She stepped away from him, breaking his hold on her. "What?"

"The minute I saw you in Tbilisi, I sort of just went crazy—"

"Crazy?"

"I can't even breathe without everything inside hurting right now. There's a giant knot in the center of my chest, and frankly, the sooner we find Josh and get you both out of the country, the better."

She got it, really she did. But it didn't make his words hurt any less. Nothing had changed at all between them. She was still a liability.

At least, however, now she knew why.

Her lips still burned from his kiss and she hated how much she longed to simply pull him back into her embrace.

"I can't believe this, but for the first time, we agree on something. I'll find Josh and this girl, and then I'll be out of your life, no problem."

She turned away, her eyes slicked with tears.

"Mae—"

She held up a hand. "Let's just get going."

"Mae, it's not like that. I just don't want the same thing happening to you that happened to Carissa."

She whirled hard. "I'm hardly spying for the government. I don't think this warlord guy is going to kill me just for hanging out with you."

Something twitched in his jaw. "He might." His eyes narrowed just for a second. Then he turned and picked up his backpack.

But she'd seen it. A flicker of fear. Terror.

"What aren't you telling me, Chet?"

"We could sure use some wheels," he said.

Oh, joy, the old Chet was back, the one who left

her out of the loop, working on a need-to-know basis. Clearly, he was done with their discussion. Fine. She'd let him off the hook—for now.

They *could* use some sort of transportation—a jeep or a motorcycle. In the field behind them, she heard a nickering. "Will four legs do?"

The dawn had just crested to the east when they found the farmer, rising to feed the scattering of chickens and goats that meandered around his fenced property. In the hills above his house, cattle lounged on the fertile table, untouched by Russian occupation. Mae held the reins of a haltered horse in her hand, having used a piece of halvah to entice the animal to come to her.

Chet did the negotiating with her dollars. It netted them a prime, fifteen-year-old black Kabardin gelding—a mountain horse—that stood politely as Mae climbed onto his bare back.

Chet stood five feet away. "Seriously? You're driving? I don't think so."

"Suit yourself. See you at the ranch, cowboy."

He shook his head, mounted a stump and got on behind her. "Don't tell me they taught you how to ride when you were in the army."

"Nope. I have no idea what I'm doing, and I like it that way. Haw!"

Mae's moods changed so fast, Chet thought he might have whiplash. He did know that for one crystal-clear second, he had felt alive. Or maybe just…hopeful. He'd actually believed that something better awaited him if he could just break free of the clutter pinning him down.

Namely, his mistakes.

Or, perhaps his still-raw emotional wounds. Which had clearly made him delirious, because he'd just about told her the entire story. The true story, not the one he had edited for his superiors almost two decades ago.

The one that haunted him, and brought him right back to the forests of central Georgia.

Sometimes there's a wound inside so deep, it can steal your breath with its completeness. At times, it feels as fresh as the day you were injured. And you wonder in that moment if God has turned away from you, horrified at your ugliness, and if it is ever possible to be whole again.

He did remember writing that to her, now.

He rubbed his chest, reliving how she, ever so briefly, slid into his arms, sweetly kissing him with more than he'd ever hoped for. Her silky hair between his fingers, her hands on his arms, her touch holding nothing back…and he'd drunk it in like a parched man. He couldn't even find words to explain why he'd done it, why he'd reached for her. Only that, for a second, he'd lost himself in her arms. Just let go and reached for her with everything inside him, exposing him for the desperate man he was.

Then, he'd opened his big stupid mouth.

Crazy. She made him *crazy*. Words to woo her with.

But being with her did stir up all kinds of crazy—like the idea that they could ride off into the sunset and live happily ever after. Right, with him leaving a trail of blood from his freshly opened wounds. Clearly wounds like his—the kind that cut to the soul—didn't heal. And he'd done his time on his knees, asking. Begging. Like Paul and his thorn.

Not that he deserved to heal. He'd resigned himself to learning how to live with the pain, however poorly he managed it. But he wasn't going to doom her to live with it, too.

"This reminds me of Washington—the rolling hills, the drape of fir trees over the hills, the smell of decaying leaves. I'll bet it's gorgeous from the air," Mae said, her voice soft in front of him.

Gorgeous, yes.

Like the picture of her moving with the gait of this beautiful animal they were riding, looking fresh and pretty under the kiss of the morning sun. He put his hands on her waist, drew in the fragrance of her long red hair as it blew against him, and listened to her travel commentary and tales of Seattle. He nearly wanted to cry with the pleasure of it. He'd already heard the story of the Great Barfer and an assortment of other catastrophes, and she'd moved on to updates on her friends Roman and Sarai, and Yanna and David, in Moscow.

If he closed his eyes, it felt almost like he was one of her letters, the news of her life like a salve.

Gorgeous, yes. Paradise.

Oh, brother. Talk about crazy.

"So, do you have a brilliant plan to find Josh when we get to Burmansk?" he asked, keeping his voice free of the panic that coiled tighter with each passing minute.

"I thought I'd start at the mission. Maybe they know where Josh liked to hang out, or where he'd go when he wasn't in camp."

"If he's trying to escape with Darya, he's probably heading toward a major city, or at least toward some sort of transportation out of the country."

"We won't know anything until we talk to his co-workers and get a read on his motives. I tried calling his teammates before I left, but the few I got hold of didn't have any idea what I was talking about. If Josh and Darya had something cooking, they kept it under the radar."

"Maybe they're holed up some place having a romantic tryst."

"Please, this is Joshy." She flashed him a look over her shoulder.

"Who is a nineteen-year-old college student! I'm being serious."

"I don't know why I talk to you."

"Sorry. Okay, how's this—maybe he's come to his senses and returned to the camp."

"Better."

He leaned forward, over her shoulder, and caught her grin. How he longed to wrap his arms around her waist, cocoon her into his embrace.

"So, does your brilliant idea include a way to talk Josh into leaving without Darya?"

She went still in front of him. "Not necessarily."

Shoot, he just had to bring that up, didn't he? Sometimes, he was his own terminator. Still, *not necessarily?* Someone needed to face reality here. "Mae, Darya's taken. We have to convince Josh that he can't be her hero."

"Do you smell smoke? Like a campfire?"

Her tone that told him that no, her plans didn't include coercing Darya into marrying against her will.

Letch.

"Look, if there's another way to solve this thing, I promise to listen, okay?" *Please, please, Mae.*

She looked back at him, hope in her beautiful eyes. "Really?"

"I'm really not a—"

"Letch? I...probably shouldn't have said that." She gave a small smile, an offering. He offered one back.

"And, yes, I smell smoke." And in fact, he saw it, too, a billow of darkness against the far horizon.

"Is that the direction of Burmansk?"

He'd been given control of the map, if not the horse, and dug it out. "Could be."

She urged their mount into a canter. "Hang on."

Just the words he'd been hoping for.

She found a deer path through the woods and had to slow to a trot but managed to keep them seated. Overhead the oaks canopied them, dappling shadow on the forest floor. He remembered the war games in these forests, teaching the rebels how to camouflage themselves, how to dig into an opportune position, how to wait for their opening. Almost on instinct, he spotted prime ambush and sniper positions.

"Let's get out of here," he said and pointed toward an opening in the forest scape. She nodded, followed a ravine out of the woods, and emerged onto a dirt road.

She reined the horse to a stop.

Chet moved his hands to her arms, holding her steady.

In the distance, at the bottom of the hill, the village burned. Flames clawed out of the windows of a building, and plumes of black smoke covered the sky, although they were too far away to see the extent of the inferno.

"Hands of Hope mission," Mae said.

"Maybe. Let's go."

Mae pushed their horse into a gallop and Chet reached around her, holding the mane, trying to keep both of them on the horse's sweaty back. As they drew closer, sirens whined, and military vans moved in and out of the smoke.

It cleared with a gust of wind, revealing villagers standing away from the flames, hands pressed to their mouths. A few pulled tattered sweaters around their bodies. Women held children to their bosoms, covering their eyes. The stench of burning rubber and wood, and molten metal, filled the air.

At the center of the chaos, a blackened two-story wooden building groaned as it was consumed. Next to it, a flatbed truck had begun to buckle.

Mae brought the horse close enough to see a

group of firefighters pumping water from an ancient truck, spitting a pitiful stream onto the building.

"I hope everyone got out," Mae said as Chet slid from the horse and reached for her.

Miraculously, she slipped into his arms. He read fear in her eyes. Josh. Chet took her hand while he had the chance.

He'd worked at a number of refugee camps during his military tours and he knew what to look for. He located someone wearing what looked like Western clothes—a pair of jeans and a sweat-shirt that said Wheaton College. College-aged, evidenced by her long blond hair pulled into a shaggy ponytail, the aid worker stared in fear as the fire roared, a living being, mesmerizing her. He touched her shoulder.

She whirled, wide-eyed.

Chet held up his hand in surrender. "Americans. We're Americans."

"What are you doing here?" She trembled, tears furrowing down her grimy cheeks. "What do you want?"

"I'm looking for someone—" Mae started, but Chet ran over her words with his.

"What happened here?"

The worker looked between them, as if not sure whom to respond to first.

She decided on Chet. "Rebel forces. Or Russians, we don't know. We just woke up this morning to a fire in our medical center. Everything's lost—the food, the medical supplies…"

Patients. The horror on her tear-streaked face told the truth.

"Is this Hands of Hope?"

She nodded. "We just got here a couple of days ago. I…I don't know what to do."

Chet glanced at Mae. Then probably she wouldn't have heard of—

"I'm looking for Josh Lund. He was an aid worker who went missing a couple of days ago. Do you know him?"

She blinked at Mae, as if trying to comprehend her words. Then she shook her head.

"You're here for Josh?" The voice came from a large woman who wore her years in her wide face. Greasy smoke smeared her cheeks as her gaze tracked to the fire behind them and back again.

"I'm his aunt," Mae said.

Great. If Mae had taken a second to consult him, instead of acting on impulse, he might have suggested leaving that tidbit of information out. Namely because of the very look the woman gave her.

As if Mae herself were responsible for the chaos her nephew had left in his wake.

"Perfect. Maybe you could explain, then, why he decided to disregard everything we've tried to do here—specifically, to stay neutral in this conflict so we can earn the trust of the locals—and instead kidnap one of the locals? What exactly is he thinking?"

Yep, Chet would have left out Mae's direct approach and gone with something a little less revealing. "I don't think Josh kidnapped her," Chet said quietly, hoping Mae got the hint. The last thing they needed here was a dash of her sarcasm to fan the flames. "I think it's a misunderstanding."

"Does this look like a misunderstanding to you, Mr.—"

"Stryker. Stryker International. I run a private security company."

See? Coming in like the good guys never hurt. People in danger liked the word *security*.

"Good, because we could use a little security here. Starting with the return of Darya to her father, who has threatened to come back in two days and burn the rest of our village to the ground if he doesn't have her. How about that for *security?*"

So, maybe that hadn't been quite the right word. "We're here to help—we'll track him down and return the girl."

He tightened his grip when Mae tried to jerk her hand away. *Calm down.*

The woman scanned Chet, then Mae. "Joyce Warner. My husband, Phil, is the director of our mission." She sighed, and the air drained from her, taking with it her anger. "Listen, we like Josh. And none of us knew who Darya was until her father showed up looking for her. Evidently, she was living with a local woman, and her father had no idea she was working at the clinic. We don't know what happened between her and Josh. Maybe he did just make a mistake. I don't know. I do know that I've heard talk of a village posse going out after him, so if you want to head that off, be my guest. I also know that if Bashim and his men return, and Josh and Darya aren't here, then we're all in big trouble."

Chet read between the lines. Josh's actions threatened the mission and the tenuous foothold peace had in this region.

He hated how well he understood every side of this fight. And what he had to do next.

"Mae, you need to stay here. If Bashim is out hunting for Josh and Darya, who knows what I'm going to find? I can't have you in the mix."

This time she did yank her hand away. "Really, this conversation needs to stop. For the hundredth time, I'm going with you." Then she held up her hand, pasted on a smile, and said, "I'm going to pretend you aren't actually speaking. Maybe that you're not even here."

Oh, for the love of Pete.

She turned to Joyce. "I will find Josh, and Darya. But I need some help. Do you know where he liked to go, or anyone who might have helped him? He's in a foreign country and doesn't speak the language—"

"Actually, he speaks it pretty well. He was taking lessons from a woman outside the village. Three mornings a week."

Screams behind them cut off Joyce's words. An outer wall of the building caved in, sparks flying onto the spectators. Villagers ran for cover.

Joyce yelled at them in Georgian.

Chet grabbed her arm before she could hustle off. "Where is this woman?"

"Outside the village," she said, pointing west, beyond Burmansk. "She's American by birth, her name is Laura. She lives in a yellow dacha about a mile from town."

Another scream, and Chet let her go.

Mae turned and headed toward their horse.

"Mae—"

"Don't do it, Chet. Besides, even if you do find Josh, if I'm not along you don't have a prayer of getting through to him."

He stopped, then caught up with her in two steps. "Why?"

She glanced at him, her lips pursed, her expression tight.

"Why, Mae?"

"Because, well, I didn't exactly like you this past year, and I may have told him how I felt, with a possible few embellishments."

He raised an eyebrow. "What did you say?"

"That you couldn't be trusted. And maybe that everything that came out of your mouth was a lie."

"A lie."

"And that you are about the most…selfish guy… I'm sorry! I was mad." Her eyes brimmed and she brushed the moisture away, almost angrily. "Smoke. Let's get out of here. We've got twenty-four hours to find him and convince him and Darya that you're not the devil."

Looking at the mud, hearing the screams, seeing the pockmarks of bullets on the village houses, knowing he'd started the war that had destroyed so many lives and homes, not to mention had put the hurt in Mae's eyes, Chet wasn't exactly sure that was possible.

SIX

Mae refused to think about the way Chet had tried to push her aside, jumped on their horse and barely pulled her up behind him.

She made a point of locking her arms around his waist.

She wouldn't put it past him to dump her out on this dirt road—his definition of "keeping her safe."

She'd seen the look in his eyes when Joyce Warner had mentioned Bashim. That same flash of *I'm-not-telling-you-but-this-is-bad* panic.

She tightened her grip on him as they moved with the gait of the cantering horse. See, they could do this, together, if he'd just let her get close enough to help—instead of constantly making it clear that he didn't want her around.

They'd left the drama of the village behind and she'd only looked back once, watching as the smoke blackened the sky and shadowed the valley in doom.

Oh, Josh, what were you thinking?

Chet still had their horse at a canter as they sank down into a valley, the terrain blotting out the village. Around them, foothills rose to rocky cliffs, scrub brush scarring the hills, backdropped by the purple mountains at the base of the mountains, leading north. In another time and place, she'd call it beautiful.

But at the moment, it just felt desolate. "Why would someone live way out here?"

She would rather live in smog-infested Beijing than a place so far from humanity. She liked her internet, her cell phone. She lived and breathed her relationships, as scattered as they were around the globe. With all this open space and no technology, she'd probably suffocate.

"I can think of a few reasons," Chet said as they topped the hill and she spotted a tiny yellow house. "Like finding the quiet of your own thoughts. Or not having someone shooting at you."

"I thought that part of your life was over."

"I hope it is."

He didn't sound as sure as she would have liked. Just how dangerous was his work? She imagined him staking out buildings, maybe guarding American diplomats. Yes, perhaps the shooting had just begun.

They slowed to a trot and then a walk as they

left the main road and followed a footpath to a stucco-yellow house about twice the size of her mother's trailer. It sat nestled in the cleft of two rising foothills covered in lush green fir. Smoke trickled from a stone chimney, and a stone well and iron pump conjured up images of a simpler way of life.

It looked as if Laura lived without indoor plumbing—another benefit of modern society Mae heartily approved of.

"Hello? Laura?" She spoke English as she and Chet dismounted, hoping to put the woman's mind at ease. No movement.

Chet tied the horse's reins to the pump. "We're just here to talk."

Still no movement behind the bright blue door. A breeze stirred a bunch of dill weed, hung upside down to dry on the porch.

"Maybe she's not here."

"Prevyet!"

The voice came from behind the house. In a moment, a woman appeared around the side, holding a basket of zucchini. *"Shto vwe hatitye?"*

"We're Americans," Mae said. "I'm looking for Josh Lund. I'm his aunt."

"Stop telling people that," Chet hissed so only she could hear. "You don't know who you can trust, or how they'll use information against you."

He turned to the woman. "Let me help you with that."

She considered him a moment, then handed him the basket, wiping a strand of long blond hair from her face, where it had escaped from her white head scarf. The wind plastered a pair of nylon pants to her skinny legs, and she drew a knee-length blue sweater, buttoned over her trim figure, tighter around her body. Mae placed her in her mid-fifties. Dirt dusted her hands up to her wrists. She squinted at Mae. "Americans?"

Chet set the basket on the porch. "Are you Laura?"

"Who's asking?" She went over to the pump next to the well and began to work the handle. Water trickled out and she washed her hands in the spray.

"I'm Mae." She looked over at Chet as she said, "I'm Josh's aunt."

Chet rolled his eyes.

"Have you seen him?"

The woman wiped her hands on a dirty towel hung over the top of the pump. "Maybe."

"Please. We're trying to help Josh. Apparently you taught him Georgian?"

The woman looked from Chet to Mae, took her basket from Chet and then turned toward her house. "Come inside. I'll make some tea."

"We don't have time—" Mae started, but Chet gave her such a nasty look that she shut her mouth and followed him into the house.

It had been built to survive time. Thick stone walls betrayed their age with crumbling mortar cracks, and the wooden floor bowed in the middle, under a threadbare woven rug.

However, the place surprised her with its warmth. A coal furnace the size of a bear jutting into the center of the room chased the chill into the corners. Atop it, a soot-blackened pot simmered, the top jiggling, pressing out steam. A knitted afghan lay wadded on a worn wooden rocker near the window, and through the bedroom doorway, a red wool blanket covered a neatly tucked double bed. In Washington, such a place would be advertised as a "rustic" getaway, and rented for two hundred dollars a night.

Laura set her basket on the long wooden table and pulled out a chair, gesturing for Chet to sit. She nodded to the other chair for Mae.

Mae met Chet's eyes as he waited, eyebrow raised, clearly waiting for her to sit.

Fine.

The minute she took her place in the chair, her stomach let out a growl.

Laura took two stained cups from a shelf over her metal sink. "You're hungry."

Mae shook her head, but Chet offered, "Maybe a little."

What, did he want to spend the next week here? She glared at him when Laura's back was turned.

Trust me, he mouthed.

Whatever.

Laura came back to the table, set down the cups, and then Chet—the "casual tourist"—opened his mouth and began to speak. In Georgian. Effectively cutting her out of the conversation. Laura listened to him, then nodded and left the room for a moment.

"What did you tell her?" Mae hissed.

Chet considered her. "That you were a little impatient. And that this child is not unlike your own son, and you were desperate to find him before he was caught and killed."

Mae glanced at Chet, her anger deflated. "You told her that?"

"You were being a little rude. I felt the need to explain."

Whose side was he on?

Laura spoke as she returned and went to the stove. "Josh used to come here a lot, with Darya. He felt comfortable here. He told me my place reminded him of a summer camp he attended when he was a kid."

Yes, the summer camp that took kids from Phoenix and sent them to the mountains. The one she'd scraped up enough to send him to each year.

Laura returned to the table, holding the steaming teapot. Balancing a small strainer filled with tea leaves over each cup, she poured the water through it. "I miss coffee, but I love Georgian tea." She smiled at Mae.

Despite herself, Mae reached out and cupped her hands around the tea, drawing it close, inhaling.

"I have some bread and cheese, too."

Laura cut them slices of homemade bread, then added to the table creamy white cheese from the icebox below the counter, a plate of *tvorog* and a saucer of raspberry jam. "For your tea."

Chet barely looked up as he inhaled the food. Now who was being rude? And to top it off, he made little sounds of enjoyment, "yums" and "wows." Laura perched on a stool at the edge of the table, picking at a piece of cheese, grinning.

She had perfect white teeth.

"Your Georgian is very good," Laura said to Chet. "I wonder, where did you learn it?"

Chet took another slice of bread. "School."

"Hmm."

Mae said nothing about Chet's lie. She should probably stop being surprised.

"How long have you lived in Georgia?" Mae asked, forcing herself to be polite.

"Nearly thirty years. I came here during college and fell in love. After my husband, Zura, died, I moved to our hunting cabin. It reminds me of him."

She rubbed her hands together, a smile that wasn't for Mae on her face. "Your nephew and his bride reminded me of us. We were so in love... and then came the war."

Chet stopped eating on the word *war*.

Mae, however, had frozen on, "Bride? They're *married?*"

"Oh, I don't know. Not yet, probably, although the way they were together, I urged them not to wait."

Chet cast Mae an *I-told-you-so* glance.

She narrowed her eyes at him. "The way they were together?"

"Clearly in love. Of course, I was ready to help them. I knew the language classes were just an excuse to be together, outside the mission. But I could see true love in their eyes, in how he wanted to protect her. It was like looking back in time to Zura."

"How long has he known her?" Chet asked, finishing off his tea.

"Only a couple of weeks, but when you meet the

one, you know." She nodded, raising an eyebrow at Mae.

The one. She couldn't look at Chet. He also kept his eyes away from her, although his mouth tightened in a dark line.

"Where did they go, Laura?" he asked quietly.

She pursed her lips. "You know, I try not to interfere with the ways here. Even if I don't agree, I hold my tongue. It's not my country. But I can't stand by and let her marry a man she doesn't love."

Oh, no. "She told you about the Iranian."

"It's barbaric."

"About half the world still conducts arranged marriages, you know. Even in America," said Chet.

Laura's eyes glittered. "I sent them to Turkey."

"Turkey?" Mae barely comprehended the word. "Turkey, as in the *country* of Turkey?"

"Well, they have to get to Chiatura first and take the train. Ideally, they'd take a flight out of Batumi—our nearest city with an airport—but the train was the safest option. They left yesterday. They probably caught today's train. They'll be out of the country by tomorrow."

"Turkey." Chet ran a hand down his face. "If we can get to Khashuri, we can intercept them—"

"Intercept them?" Laura's hospitality vanished with her tone. "Why?"

"Because she's Akif Bashim's daughter," Chet said quietly.

Laura paled, the name making an impact that Mae couldn't feel. The older woman scrutinized Chet with a gaze, clearly contemplating something. Then she said, "Oh. My. You're *him*."

Him?

Mae glanced at Chet, who had frozen. His hand touched hers under the table.

"I don't know—"

"Code name Pancho?"

Her eyes turned obsidian, her mouth a tight knot of what looked like fury.

Chet got up. "We have to go if we hope to intercept them."

"You *are* him, aren't you?"

"I don't know what you're talking about." Chet pulled Mae up from her chair. "Thank you for the tea."

Mae looked from Laura to Chet. "Wait—"

Laura caught Mae's hand. "You may find your nephew, but your boyfriend will never leave this country alive."

"Now, Mae. We're leaving now."

She shook out of his grip, rounding on Laura. "What isn't he telling me?" And the very fact that she had to ask this woman—that Laura knew more about Chet than Mae—burned a hole right through the center of her chest.

And through the last remnants of her hope that he'd ever really trust her.

Laura kept her eyes on Chet. "Pancho is the name of Georgia's number-one enemy. American. Six foot two. Dark hair, blue eyes. The leader who armed our country for a civil war. The one we're still fighting, by the way." She yanked the scarf from her head. Along the side of her temple, an ugly rumpled red swath of skin parted her hair. "I got this from a grenade as my husband and I tried to escape Gori. I survived."

Mae stared at the hideous scar, unable to speak. She glanced at Chet. He stood hard-jawed, motionless, looking away, out the window.

Code name Pancho?

"You can't blame him for the actions of a nation," Mae tried, hearing but not believing her own voice. Even on autopilot, she rose to defend her friends.

But really, he'd stopped being a friend about five minutes ago.

Who, in fact, was Chet Stryker? Enemy? Rescuer?

Victim. He turned toward her, shame in his eyes.

Laura raised a thin brow. "You can't blame a

man for the actions of a nation? Really? Because Akif Bashim does. He's got a shoot-to-kill order out on Pancho, and a nice hefty price on Pancho's head, one that about half the country—no, make that the majority, thanks to the scars he left behind—would like to cash in on."

"Are you done?" Chet snapped.

Mae had gone cold, right to her toes. Chet grabbed her by the arm. "Thanks again for the tea," he growled, and hauled her out the door.

"A price. Did she say a *price?*"

"Just calm down." At least Mae had decided to speak to him again. Chet should probably be happy for that fact.

Maybe.

Except that she'd buried her fingers in his upper arms as she held on to him, and it sort of hurt.

Along with her tone. "I *cannot* believe you left that little tidbit out. Not only are you in a country that gives you nightmares, but you are *wanted.* By a terrorist. Who will pay money to have you killed! Did I leave anything out?"

"How about, I just wanted to protect you. I thought if you were worried about me, well, then you wouldn't focus on Josh. And I didn't want you to get upset."

"Well, I'm unfocused and plenty worried.

And upset. Wow, am I *upset.* How's that strategy working for you now?"

He closed his mouth. Shoot.

"I can't believe… You know, I just *knew* you weren't telling me everything, Chet. But I sort of thought it might be something like, I don't know, that you were married once before. Had a wife or something. Something, maybe, normal in the scope of real society. But no, you're *wanted by a terrorist.* You've got a price on your head. Someone is going to shoot you, and you'll die in my arms."

In her arms?

"Mae—"

"Let's just find Josh." Her voice sounded strange, as if she might be trying not to cry. "And Darya. And get them both to safety. And then I promise, I'll walk out of your life, and you won't need to worry about trying to protect me or upsetting me. You can just go on living in your private world, telling me only the information you think I want to hear."

"Yeah, well, I'm pretty sure you wouldn't like the unedited me." He didn't care that the sharp edge of his tone might cut her.

She gasped, loosening her grip on his arm.

Okay, maybe he did care.

"Is that what you think?"

It was what he knew. Because if she knew the

real Chet, and the crimes he hid—the ones committed right here in Georgia… No, he liked her thinking of him as the person he'd created for her. He, in fact, liked that person better, too.

He cleared his throat of the emotion rising inside him. "Chiatura is west of here, about a day's ride on these roads. If we can get a car, we can probably intercept the train. It doesn't travel fast, and if we go south, we can probably catch it up in Khashuri. Luckily, that's outside the no-man's land of South Ossetia."

She said nothing for a long while. Finally, in a voice that trembled just slightly, she said, "Clearly, it doesn't matter where we go. You have enemies on both sides of the border, Pancho."

He winced. "Thank you for pointing that out. And you can stop with 'Pancho.' It was a call sign, not a nickname."

"What's it stand for?"

"Nothing. Just…"

"Pancho Villa, maybe? The rebel leader?"

"No."

"Then what?"

"Stop please, Mae. No one is going to recognize me—"

"Are you kidding me? We had tea with one— count 'em, one—Georgian woman!" Her voice rose to anger again and lost all traces of pity. He wasn't sure which tone he preferred. "And yet she knew exactly who you were and could be on her way to warn this Bashim guy right now. I half expected a shot in my back as we rode away."

"She wouldn't have shot you," he said quietly. Although fear nearly choked him at the thought. Yes, it would be just his luck that he'd live and she'd get caught in the cross fire.

Just like Carissa.

Don't go there.

Mae held tighter as he urged the horse into a canter. "No, you're right. She would have just shot *you*." She made a little disgusted noise that tightened his gut. "Big, big difference. Puh-*lease*." He could feel the top of her head resting against his spine. "What was I thinking?"

So he'd been right. She'd gotten a good, up-close look at him, and it only made her sick.

He tried to swallow back the acid in his throat, his wild hopes of mending their friendship—or whatever it was between them—dashed.

Shoot.

"Let's see if we can get some wheels. I think our ride here has about had it."

She said nothing as they trotted toward Burmansk, and left their ride just outside town with a local farmer.

A few blocks into town, they unearthed a rusty

white Lada parked next to a charred house, weeds folding over the hood. Chet cleared the grass from the tires. They looked firm, but they'd recessed into the dirt. "It looks like it's been here a couple of years."

Mae opened the gas tank and took a whiff. "Ew. It smells like paint thinner. I'm not sure this gas is good. If it even starts, it'll run rough."

Chet opened the door and slipped into the front seat. "Let's see if she'll start." Of course, no key dangled in the ignition. He checked the visor, the ashtray—nothing. And the steering was locked. Thankfully, the steering column lay exposed— good, practical Russian engineering—and a single nut held the steering wheel tight.

"You don't have your Leatherman, do you?"

She handed him the tool through the window. "Pop the hood," she said.

He reached in under the dash and released the latch with a click. Mae eased the hood open, the metal whining against her efforts while he found the power wires, exposed them, then touched them to the starter wire. He heard a click.

At least the battery had a hint of life.

"I checked the oil, and the radiator has fluid, but the distributor cap is loose," Mae said from under the hood.

He got out and found her checking the greasy

wires. "They might have been in a hurry to leave—"

"Or something else happened." She nodded toward the house. Fire had scorched the windows, char spreading out from the broken panes, and at least half the roof lay inside on the floor.

She lifted off the distributor cap. "The rotor is corroded and the spark can't get to the plugs. Let's see if I can clean the corrosion off. Then maybe we can get this thing started."

She snapped off the rotor and scraped the tip on a rock nearby, as if she were filing it. Then she snapped it back on.

Reaching along the lip of the hood, she unlatched a small pouch.

"What's that?"

"Tool kit." She opened it. Inside lay a pair of pliers, a screwdriver and a spark-plug wrench.

"Handy."

"Oh, those Russians are always thinking ahead."

She took out the flathead screwdriver and scraped the metal terminals inside the distributor cap.

"You're pretty handy, too."

She ignored him. So much for making friends.

She put the assembly back together, then stuck her hand down beside the carburetor.

"What are you doing?"

"On these old Russian cars, there's a lever on the side of the fuel pump." As she said it, she began to pump.

"Want me to do that?"

She ignored him. "Let's see if it will fire. It's got fuel, and it should have spark and I cleaned out the carburetor so it'll have air."

She wore a mark of grease on her chin, and it took everything inside him to refrain from wiping it off. But he had to admit a swell of pride at her mechanical abilities.

And shame over so quickly dismissing them.

He sorted through his memory of Russian engineering. "This is one of those crank starts, right?"

She leaned over the front, pushing away the tall grass. "Looks like it."

"Let's see if we can crank it over." He opened the trunk and took out the tire jack. "Put this in there."

Mae took it from him and fitted the jack in the crank. She gave it a turn. Nothing.

Another turn. Not even a cough.

"Are you sure you checked the spark plugs?"

She cranked again, giving him a dark look. "Just let me work here."

"Maybe I should crank."

She held up the tire iron. He stepped back, hands up. "Let me know if you need me."

Her beautiful red hair fell over her face as she gave it another good round. The engine popped once. Sputtered. Died.

"Are you sure you don't want to let me have a whirl?"

She glanced up at him and sighed. "Fine, grease monkey, have at it." She handed him the jack. "Clearly, I'm just in the way."

She leaned against the side of the car, arms folded while he gave it a good crank. The engine popped again.

"You know, I was just trying to—"

"I know, protect me."

He turned the crank again. It was harder than it looked. "I don't know what's...so...bad about that."

She shook her head. "You know, I probably wouldn't be so angry about your not telling me about your outlaw status if it didn't prove my initial assumptions. You don't respect me."

"What? Where do you get that?"

She air quoted her next words. "'I can't let you fly for me. It's too risky.'"

He clenched his jaw as he cranked.

"And then there's the 'Don't go to Georgia, Mae, you'll just get hurt.'"

"There's a war going on, if you hadn't noticed."

"How about the small matter of the need-to-know basis?"

"Plausible deniability."

"Whatever. And then, of course, there's 'I'm pretty sure you wouldn't like the unedited me.' Do you really think I'm that shallow? That I expect you to be without scars or flaws? When did I ever give you that impression?"

He couldn't look at her. Because, well, she hadn't given him that impression. Ever.

He'd taken a good look at himself and made that call all on his own.

"The truth hurts, but it all boils down to the fact that you can't bear to let me make my own decisions. You feel compelled to protect me, which makes me feel about three years old and hardly allows for teamwork, let alone respect."

"We're a team now."

"I'd hoped we could get there. But apparently not. Because you have to be able to trust your teammate. And clearly we also have issues in that area, too, because people who trust each other tell each other the truth."

"I trust you," he muttered. He cranked again, sweat beading on his forehead. The car popped and shook, and for a second, caught.

"Give it some gas—"

Mae was already inside pumping.

The car died.

"Crank it again."

He turned, hard, and the car growled to life, popping, sputtering, coughing. "Sounds like the timing is off. Hear that pinging?"

"It's just the old fuel. But it'll run."

"I'll push you out of the weeds if you put it in Reverse. But please don't drive away on me."

A dangerous look glimmered in her eye.

Maybe he didn't trust her after all.

But, miracle of miracles, she waited for him as he muscled the car out of its moorings. She didn't, however, climb into the passenger seat to let him drive.

They took off down the road, her jaw tight, her hands white on the steering wheel.

Sheesh, did a guy have to tell a woman everything? Did she require him to open up his chest and reveal his entire life story?

He had his reasons for all of his decisions— keeping her in the dark, not involving her in his company—and they were good ones, too. A couple even had to do with her.

As he watched her manhandle the car up the rutted dirt road, it occurred to him that she hadn't, *not once,* asked for his help. At least not since he'd set foot in the country.

"Listen, sweetheart, it goes both ways here. You want to be on a team, but that means you have to trust *me,* too. Even when you don't have all the facts. The truth is, you always have to be in charge, always have to save the day. But—and brace yourself because the truth hurts—sometimes you get in over your head, Mae. It's like you don't even *care* what happens to you. How many times have I watched your pal David sink to his knees in white-knuckle prayer, hoping you won't get killed? You're impulsive and—"

"Hey, my impulsiveness has saved lives—"

"—reckless, too. Could it be I was just watching your back?"

"I don't want anyone to watch my back."

"Clearly. Especially a man."

She shot him a look, but he knew he'd touched on the truth.

"And why is that, Mae? I'm just wondering, because suddenly I'm thinking I'm not the only one who may have edited myself a little. Why do you always have to save the day? Why can't you let people help you? Why does it scare you so much to rely on me? I don't think I'm the only one who hit the eject button in Moscow, Mae."

"That's not fair. You said you didn't want me."

"I didn't want you to *work* for me. As I recall, you filled in the rest."

She blinked, and a tear spilled down her cheek. She didn't even bother to wipe it away as they drove past the smoking mission and south along the road to Khashuri.

SEVEN

"Are you trying to take out the axles, or are you just unfamiliar with actually having tires on the ground?"

Mae ignored him. Although that last bump… well, she may have banged her head on the roof.

They'd escaped the war zone, with the Russian soldiers scurrying over the hills and the carnage of war—burned houses, the road churned to rubble— everywhere. In a few sections, she'd had to veer off the road to traverse the mess. It took longer than she'd hoped and the sun was practically swan-diving into the horizon, washing the car in gloom.

Why do you always have to save the day?

Chet's words thrummed in her head, even as she wrangled the car around potholes, sweat slicking her back. *Why does it scare you so much to rely on me?*

Because he'd let her down, that was why. Because that was just how she was built—men disappointed her. It was like some sort of defect in her programming. Regardless of what she did, or probably because of everything she didn't do—like fawn over them and call them her hero—once they got close enough, they turned and ran. Like Olympic sprinters.

Take Chet, for example. Or Vicktor, her college boyfriend. No, she and Viktor, although they'd been in a study group together in Moscow University, had never been a good match—not with their first-born mentalities. She never did understand why her friend David set her up with his roommate Vicktor. And, seeing him with Gracie, the way she allowed him to rescue her—to save her from a serial killer, and even a human trafficker in Seattle—yes, Gracie and Vicktor managed to find true love.

Mae wasn't sure she'd recognize if it tackled her to the ground. Not that she'd stick around long enough to get caught. Her father taught her that.

Chet came alive beside her. "The way I figure it, we'll hook up with the train just north of Kashuri. There's a little village about twenty miles from here where it makes a pit stop. We can sneak in there and jump aboard while the passengers are disembarking for roadside goodies."

"I used to love that tradition," Mae said, keeping her voice light, as if she weren't still reeling from his accusations. "When I'd travel to Khabarovsk, where Vicktor lived, sometimes we'd take a train to Vladivostok. It would stop in all these tiny villages, and we'd buy fresh *vareniki* or a delicious torte filled with caramel."

"Stop, you're making me hungry."

Chet sat with one foot braced against the floorboard, his right hand iron-fisted around the door handle. He had long since stopped trying to hold in his grunts when she managed to bottom out the car in a pothole, or slam him against the door in an attempt to avoid said potholes.

Yes, she missed the sky. Her plane.

In fact, she'd do just about anything to be airborne right now. Alone.

Just her at the controls of her plane, no one telling her—

"Sheesh, Mae! Do you think I could keep my teeth on this trip?"

She wrenched the wheel around the next pothole. "Sorry."

He sighed beside her. "I guess I wouldn't be doing any better. It's not like this road is made for travel over thirty-five miles an hour."

"I'm going thirty."

"Right." He gave a small chuckle.

"What's so funny?"

"Oh, I was thinking about Artyom and his lousy driving. He's this new guy I hired—"

"I know him. He helped us break Roman out of the gulag."

He glanced at her. "I'd forgotten about that. He posed as one of the guards."

"Along with David." Who, although he was supposed to have been working undercover in an undisclosed country, went off the radar long enough to help his best friend escape death. Something the army had conveniently never discovered.

As if Mae could read his mind, she asked, "What were you doing when David was rescuing Roman?"

Chet chuckled under her breath. "Trying to keep his junket off the books. We were supposed to be meeting with high-and-mighties in D.C. about our next mission. I show up at David's apartment only to discover that he's AWOL. Not even a note. I got hold of him in Anchorage, right before—"

"He met me. We took a cargo flight to Khabarovsk, then another to Siberia. He never let on that he was on a mission."

"He didn't have to. I had his back."

I had his back. Chet said those words so easily, but they opened another rip inside. No one had been back home in Alaska watching *her* back, keeping her name below the radar. No, she'd returned home to a near court martial. Only the fact she'd been on leave had kept her from ending up at Leavenworth.

In fact, she wasn't sure anyone had *ever* had her back.

Her realization should have been accompanied by dramatic music, because at once, she saw her life in a wide-angle view. She didn't see any of her friends—Roman, David, Vicktor, even Yanna—rushing to Georgia to help her find her nephew. No, they all had lives. Or better sense than to risk their lives for a love-struck teenager. And his over-zealous aunt.

No, only she dropped everything and ran off to save the world.

The truth hurts. Maybe she did have a savior complex.

Her eyes blurred, and she wrenched the wheel again before she hit another bump.

Chet slid his hand over her arm. "I can drive if you want."

She gritted her teeth and looked down at his hand. Gentle, firm. Capable.

Chet. Chet had dropped everything and come to Georgia to help her.

Why did you come back? Her words, shouted at him in the woods only this morning—wow, it felt like a couple of lifetimes ago—barraged her.

You can't figure that out, Mae?

She hadn't really let herself think about the fact that he'd kissed her—oh, how he'd kissed her. And that she'd responded with more of herself than she should have.

For a blink in time, in his arms she felt…safe. So safe. As if she could breathe out, uncoil the failures and fears that held her so tight some days she thought she might suffocate. For that second, she felt as if she didn't have to rush in and save the day, as if she might be enough, just as she was. Without her red cape.

She glanced at Chet's hand on her arm, then up at his face. He was watching her with those devastating blue eyes that seemed to be able to see right through her, all the way to the fear inside—of not being needed.

He looked tired and a little bit on edge, with the husk of whiskers on his face, and dirt on his denim shirt and the knees of his black jeans.

She tapped the brakes and scooted over to the side of the road.

"What are you doing?" He pulled his hand away as she put the car into Park.

"Would you like to drive?"

"Are you serious? This isn't because you're angry about my side-seat driving is it?"

She rubbed her aching hands on her pant legs. Fatigue suddenly pouring through her, and not only from the past three days, but maybe from the past three decades. She swallowed and shook her head. "I'm not mad at you. I'm just….ready to let you drive."

If she wasn't mistaken, a smile edged up the side of his face—something sweet, especially when she factored in the strange, almost compassionate expression in his eyes. "Okay, then. Scoot over, baby. Chet Stryker's at the wheel."

Mae was letting him drive. She was *letting* him drive.

Ho-kay, it wasn't as if he'd been asked to guard the president, or won a peace prize or saved the world from nuclear disaster. But it felt as if he had.

Miss *Get-outta-my-way-while-I-save-humanity* was letting him *drive*.

And she'd hadn't once freaked out about it or hovered over him, gritting her teeth as he—yes, it seemed the potholes actually opened up under his tires—bounced them through pocks in the road.

"Sorry," he said as the car squealed, righting itself.

She had reclined the seat, folded her arms across her chest and closed her eyes. "I still have my teeth," she said.

What happened? The last coherent thing he'd said to her—right before losing his temper and decimating his hopes that she'd ever talk to him again—was something about how she scared him with her savior tactics, how she always had to be the boss, how he longed for her to be his teammate…or maybe that last part was just a conversation he'd had in his head…

Good grief, the woman got a rusty old car running. It's about time you woke up and started realizing you need her.

And so what do I do—hand her a gun, let her blaze away as Akif and his thugs hijack us?

She's probably got pretty good aim, having been in the military for over a decade.

And what happens when she gets shot—or worse, Akif gets his grubby paws on her?

Sadly, that was where the conversation ended, with a fear so powerful it nearly devoured him whole.

Yes, that was about when he'd unraveled and blasted her with the part of him who could really be a jerk. He'd even made her cry. What a hero.

Now, as he glanced at her, her red hair down— she'd pulled it out of the ponytail to lean back in the seat—her body drifting into sleep, he continued his earlier train of thought.

So Akif grabs her. She's pretty tough. Are you so sure she can't take care of herself? She did wallop you hard.

Fine. Then what? We live through whatever Akif throws at us...and ride off into happily-ever-after?

Silence. Yep, that was right. He didn't get past there, ever. He was just left with a yearning so overwhelming it nearly brought tears to his eyes.

Happily-ever-after. He didn't even know what that might mean anymore.

Happily-ever-after might mean finding Josh on the train, and convincing Mae to tag along with her nephew to the safety of Turkey, or at least to some westernized country while he backtracked with Darya to Burmansk. Maybe it also included Chet sneaking out of the country without getting killed by Akif. And then what?

What?

Maybe...maybe he called Mae and asked her to move to Prague. So they could...?

He glanced at her. She'd never be happy unless she was flying. And she deserved to fly. She'd earned her wings over and over, and yes, she was probably the best pilot he'd ever find.

So, maybe happily-ever-after was figuring out a way to forget the past and start over.

Carissa's scream jerked through him and he slammed his hand on the steering wheel, trying to clear his head.

Next to him, Mae opened her eyes. "You okay?"

"Yeah," he said, keeping his gaze forward, willing away the memory of her being torn from his arms, her pleading cries as—

"Hey, is that Gori?" Mae pointed to a village in the distance, now coming into view as they huffed to the top of the hill.

"I think so. It's the next stop on the map. We'll pick up the train there."

"I hope you have some lari left, because buying Argo cashed me out."

"Argo?"

"Our horse. It's the name of Xena's horse, on *Xena: Warrior Princess*."

"Seriously? Are you kidding me?"

She smiled at him. "I have every season on DVD."

"Of course you do." He glanced at her with a smirk.

"What? There's a lot more depth there than you'd think. Good versus evil, friendship—"

"Women who are stronger than men."

"Sometimes they are."

"I think the men are just distracted by her outfit."

Mae rolled her eyes, but she smiled. "Okay,

maybe she has some issues, but I did like the horse."

"I thought he was more of a Silver."

"As in 'Hi-Ho Silver, away'? Oh, good grief. And who was I then, Tonto?"

"Well, actually, I thought I might be Tonto."

"Which makes me the…Lone Ranger."

Her tone told him his words still burned in her mind.

He made a face, looking over at her. "I'm sorry. That probably wasn't fair."

She lifted a shoulder. "Maybe it was. You might be right, you know…about what you said."

He stared straight ahead, nearly holding his breath.

"Don't get your hopes up that I'm going to hop the first train for the border."

Shoot. That was exactly what he'd been hoping for.

"But I see your point. I do that—drop everything, rush to fix things. Maybe I just can't get past the fear that maybe I just *think* they need me."

"And they really don't?" He said it softly, and now glanced at her. She was looking away from him, out the window, but as he watched, she wiped a hand across her cheek.

Perfect. He'd made her cry again. "Mae—"

"No, you're right. That's…well, yeah. I am afraid

they won't need me. That somehow they'll forget about me, or maybe just go on without me."

"Like Gracie did. When she married Vicktor and moved to Prague. Or I did." Oh, he got it now. Watching her friends, her family, go on with their lives, reach for their dreams, while hers did a slow spiral into a ugly crash.

"Or my father did." She was staring at her hands, folding them into each other in her lap.

Her father?

"He left when I was ten. Just walked out the door of our trailer. I stood there, my feet bare on the metal steps, freezing to death in my flimsy night-gown. I think it was even raining. I watched him throw a paper bag of his clothing into the cab of his truck and climb in. He never looked back."

"Mae—"

"The worst part about it was that my mother hadn't come home the night before. I hadn't done the dishes, and when he came home from his shift around midnight, he was furious. It took me years to figure out that he was angry at her, but of course I thought it was me. I'd let him down. He worked so hard and was always grumbling about how much his ungrateful family cost him. I know now he meant my mother, but as a ten-year-old, I couldn't tell the difference. I never felt like he really liked me, or my sister. When he left, there was a part of me that felt relief.

"Only then my mother started bringing home her perverted boyfriends. It really made me miss him. Even with all his complaining, he had never scared me, never made me feel like I had to lock my door at night. I left as soon as I could."

His imagination had caught on "perverted." Little explosions of fury ignited in his chest.

No wonder she had a little trouble trusting men.

And then there was that minor detail of him cutting her out of his life. *Good move, Chet.* He wanted to howl. "I'm so sorry I made you feel like a burden, Mae."

"It's not your fault. You get to choose your own life, without me dragging along behind—"

"You'd hardly be dragging, Mae. I just… Okay, fine, the thought of you getting hurt, and having it be my fault, was just too big. Every time I thought about it, it nearly doubled me over. I can't be responsible for someone's death again."

Even as he said it, as the words tumbled out of his mouth, he felt the past balling up in his chest, aching to boil out.

He took a long breath.

She stared at him. "You're talking about Carissa, aren't you?"

He clamped his jaw tight but nodded. Maybe it was time for the truth. It couldn't really get worse could it? She already thought him a lost cause. She'd all but said as much just hours ago. *What was I thinking?*

He had no answer for that. Why had Mae given him a second look, let him talk her into escaping Gracie's party with him? Beautiful Mae, who laughed at his jokes and twined her long fingers through his and let him pull her close and bury his face in her hair? What was she thinking?

Do you really think I'm that shallow? That I expect you to be without scars or flaws?

He cleared his throat and took a deep breath. "Yes, I'm talking about Carissa."

"She was more than just an operative, wasn't she? More than a teammate?" Mae had turned in her seat toward him.

He couldn't look at her. "How did you know?"

"Give me some credit for reading between the lines. You loved her," she said, her voice gentle.

You loved her. Those words seemed too simple, not enough for the feelings he'd had for Carissa. His love for her had consumed him, swept common sense from his brain. He would have gone to the edge of death and back for her.

He had, in fact. "Yes."

Mae put her hand on his arm, as if steadying him. "What really happened, Chet?"

He tapped the brakes as he moved his hand off the steering wheel and took hers. They had entered the village, motoring past fences that looked like skewers in the ground, loose and wobbling in the wind. Dogs scattered, barking at their car.

So much for not calling attention to themselves.

He drew a breath. "She was my contact at the Georgian embassy in Gori. It was only after a couple months of her feeding us information about the Georgian army that I realized she was the daughter of the Ossetian warlord—Akif Bashim. And of course, he was the one who sent us in her direction. He placed her in the embassy as a maid, then used her as a test to see if we could truly be trusted. Which, of course, we could. Except for the fact that I was young and stupid, and had fallen for Carissa, hard." He glanced at her hand, her fingers now laced through his. "I actually envisioned, after the fighting started, stealing her away to safety where we could be married, and start a life."

She still hadn't let go of his hand.

"I was a fool. And I lost my grip on my priorities. Worse, I didn't realize that Akif knew about us. She snuck out one night, to the village where I had found a room, and we spent the night together."

Mae didn't react even to his words.

It wasn't until years later, when he'd met David Curtiss and encountered his partner's faith that Chet realized how much of himself he'd given to Carissa in sleeping with her before marriage. Perhaps, in a way, it was that act that made his wounds so deep, so unable to heal. The fact that he'd betrayed her faith…and her honor, not to mention his own.

"I woke to the sound of his AK-47 being chambered. And Carissa's scream as Akif's men yanked her from our bed." He tried to breathe past the burn in his throat. "Her father took us out of the village and his men beat her—" his voice barely managed a whisper "—while he made me watch."

She was silent next to him. Painfully silent. He pulled up to the train station in the center of town. As he turned off the car, he took in the street traffic, the array of hometown vendors lined up with tables or standing by the tracks.

They'd beat the train.

He glanced at her, about to announce this news, but she was still back in the story, caught there. She had both hands holding his now, her eyes full, a tear dripping off her chin. She didn't even bother to wipe it as it plopped onto her pants. "Did they kill her?"

He nodded.

"Thankfully, I was too… I was pretty worked over by then. I didn't have to watch her die."

Mae squeezed his hands, another tear dripping onto her cheek. "I'm sorry."

He tore his gaze away. "It's in the past."

She blinked at his words, her amazing green eyes darkening. "It's *not* in the past. It's here."

She moved her hand to the chain around his neck, touching it. "It's right here between us. It's why you can't bear to have me fly for you. And why you keep wanting to send me packing. It's why, last night, you had a nightmare, and why you look like you're going to combust every second you're in Georgia."

He glanced at her, then back at the babushkas trolleying metal milk canisters down the rutted dirt road toward the station, and at the children on bicycles, laughing…

No, it wasn't in the past. And clearly, he couldn't break free of it either, despite the years of dodging and hoping and praying and wishing.

He reached up and wiped away the tear that lay on her cheek. She didn't pull away.

He took her hand, kissed it and put it back on her lap. "It's why we need to get on that train and get Josh, and why I need you to walk away from me. Not because I want you to, but because you should."

She looked at him with a sort of dark horror on her face.

"I don't want to lose you, Mae, I really don't." Oh, no, his voice was breaking. He closed his mouth, shook his head. *Get a hold of yourself.* Still, he did feel like he *might* combust, right there, he might even cry with the bubble of pain building in his chest. But he owed her the truth, and he'd come this far...

"The truth is, I know that if you see how desperately I need you, it'll scare you back to your senses. You'll realize that I'm just a guy who's made mistake after mistake, and who will probably only get you killed. And because of that, and because I'm so incredibly selfish, I need you to walk away from me."

"Chet, you're hardly selfish—"

"Let me finish, because you don't quite get it." He couldn't look at her so he held on to the wheel and hung his head. "I *am* selfish. I'm so scared of losing you that I'm willing to tell you that I don't love you. That I want you to stay far, far away from me, and that you can't be in my life, even though it's completely unfair to *you,* because it's too risky for *me.*"

"Chet—"

"And that's why I rejected you in Prague, and didn't write for a year, and yes, even why I left out some of the darker parts of myself from my letters. Because I—"

"Was afraid that I might love you?"

"No, because I *wanted* you to love me. Back. Wanted you to love me *back*."

Oh, he'd said it. He loved her.

And, of course, he had to look at her then. She stared at him with those incredible green eyes, so much hope and vulnerability and sweetness on her face—and just like that, the scabs ripped off, everything exposed to the air, burning, open, raw and, oh, what was he *thinking?*

But there was more and she had to know it before she started handing out pieces of her own heart. "See, you were right back there in the village, Mae. I don't want you to make your own choices. I want to choose for you, because if I don't, I'm doomed."

He watched as his words registered in her eyes, confusion passing over her face like a shadow.

He didn't wait for an answer. He opened the door and jumped out of the car, because, as if suddenly God had decided to take sides, the train rolled into the station.

EIGHT

He loved her?

Chet Stryker *loved* her?

Except, Mae didn't quite get that last part about being doomed. *I want to choose for you, because if I don't, I'm doomed.*

Doomed? As in, condemned, without hope?

Clearly, she didn't speak Chet Stryker.

Not that she had time to interpret his words, not with Chet's hand wrapped around hers, pulling her in a quick walk down the railroad platform past the grimy red and silver train cars and passengers loading on their suitcases. Dogs were slinking around, hoping for a scrap from scarf-wrapped peasants selling boiled potatoes and walnuts to passengers. Oh, no. To add to her problems, her stomach roared to life.

"Can we grab something to eat?"

"We gotta get on the train, Mae," Chet growled, nearly under his breath. He dodged passengers now disembarking. "Find a conductor who's distracted."

Right. Because like a fleet of soldiers, the green-coated conductors stood outside the door, waiting for stowaways like her. And Chet.

He pushed her toward a space between an elderly woman and a little girl who had stopped to talk to the conductor. The conductor, a doughy woman kneaded into her uniform, bent to talk to the pig-tailed girl.

Chet's hands circled Mae's waist as he hoisted her up the steps. He pushed in behind her and kept his hand on the small of her back as he turned her toward the inner door and pulled it open. "Let's hope there's an empty compartment in this car."

"How are we going to find Josh?"

"Let's get inside first, then we'll come up with a plan. We can't just go from car to car, poking our heads into compartments."

Laura's words in Mae's memory stopped the *Why not?* breaching her lips. *You may find your nephew, but your boyfriend will never leave this country alive.*

Right. Wanted. *Price.* And every time Chet stuck his head into an unknown compartment, well, there lurked the not-so-unlikely possibility he might get it chopped off.

She let him maneuver her down the aisle,

peeking into compartments for one that might be empty. The train reeked of baked vinyl, dust and way too much unwashed body. Or maybe that was just her own three-day smell rising up to offend her.

Chet directed her into an empty compartment with the upper red vinyl bunks still secured in their stowaway position and the table between the two lower benches flattened against the wall. Turning, he shoved the door shut, braced his hands on it and breathed hard, just for a moment. She wanted to smooth her hand down his back, right below his neck where his muscles were strung tight.

But, well, his word continued to ring in her head. Doomed, he'd said. *Doomed.*

And to think, for a second there, she'd *thought* he said he loved her.

The train whistled. Chet scraped a hand down his face. "Okay, we need to come up with a plan."

"I want to know what you meant by 'doomed.'"

An expression of panic crossed his face, his eyes opening wide before he blew out a breath and sank down on the bench. He rubbed his fingertips against his forehead, as if working out the stress.

"I don't under—" she started.

"Because if you loved me—even though I hoped for it, practically prayed for it—I also knew that you were the kind of person who would...do... something crazy."

Some sort of thunderclap should have accompanied the "aha" that resounded in her brain. "You added up my—what did you call it? *Impulsiveness*—with your past, and it equaled Mae doing something stupid to save your life."

He lifted his eyes to hers, and the pain in them jarred her. She sank down on the seat, palmed her hands against the hot vinyl.

Bingo.

"Wow, you must really think I'm out there, in left field, desperate for a man."

He flinched. "No, Mae, c'mon—"

She couldn't believe she'd told him all that about her father, and her fear of being left behind, of people forgetting her. "No, maybe not a man, but desperate to be loved, or liked."

"Mae..."

Shoot, running through the words in her mind, it did sort of sound like that. She was desperate for people to need her.

To love her.

She winced, looked out the window as the train lurched forward with a jerk. Chet put a hand to her shoulder, but she shrugged it off.

"Well, don't worry. I don't."

"You don't what?"

She looked right at him. Her voice turned tight, crisp, even through her constricting throat. "Love you."

He stared at her, a muscle twitching in his cheek. Then he drew in a breath, his expression hard. "Good."

"Good."

"Let's find Josh." He got up and turned away—and just in time. She pressed her fingertips to her eyelids to hold back the tears.

Good. She wouldn't want him to be doomed, after all.

The train conductor had already started to bump her way down the aisle, stopping at compartments to check tickets, as Chet pushed Mae out ahead of her and into the next car.

"What's the plan?" Mae asked as they paused in the opening between cars. The wind ran through his hair, stole her voice. Chet turned, grabbing her shoulders, his breath in her ear. And of course, a little tingly jolt of rebelliousness went through her when his lips touched her neck.

No, she didn't love him. And she certainly hoped her heart had gotten that memo. Because it was too dangerous for *him*.

She'd have to agree with him—maybe he *was* a little selfish.

"We need to go through each car, get behind a

conductor, and peek into the compartments without anyone noticing."

As he said it, as she watched the conductor waddle away through the rectangular glass window, she knew what to do.

"Don't follow too close," she said over her shoulder as she slipped inside the next car, noted that the conductor was halfway down the aisle, and ducked into the women's vacated compartment.

Chet, of course, couldn't obey, and moved in right behind her. "What are you do—"

She held up one finger, pressing it to her lips. Then she opened the tiny utility closet in the conductor's room and shifted through the attire until she unearthed a blue coat, almost like a bathrobe. "The cleaning people use them," she whispered. She grabbed a pillow and pulled the case off, wrapping it around her head, tying it in the back. Then she lifted a tray and a large white teapot filled with *kepitoke,* or tea concentrate, from the hot plate. Out in the main galley, a samovar steamed, filled with hot water.

"You're not thinking of passing yourself off as a tea lady, are you?" Chet said, barring the door with his body. She put a hand to his sternum and handed him her bag.

"Yes, I am, thanks."

"Please, Mae, we can figure out another way. Don't do this—"

She raised an eyebrow, wanting to push him aside, maybe drop a few choice words about how he had given up the right to tell her what to do. But she could read pain in his eyes and couldn't bear to twist the knife.

She put her hand on his chest, felt his hammering heart, and gently pushed past him into the hall. "All you have to do is hang out about ten feet away and stare out the window. I'll be fine. You don't know what Josh looks like, anyway."

"But I know what Darya looks like."

She flinched. Darya, the younger sister of the girl he'd loved. As opposed to her, the girl who got in the way. "All the more reason to stay back. What if she knows you? What if your picture is up at camp with a target on it? What if she recognizes you? You don't know what she'll do."

She had a point, and it registered on his face. He cleared his throat, turned his back to her and affected a casual pose as he leaned against the railing and stared out at the landscape chugging by.

Ah, cooperation, she'd almost forgotten what that looked like.

Please, God, help me find Joshy. She hadn't exactly been praying her way through the past couple days, but she and God were beyond need-to-know. He knew it all.

Including the fact that she *didn't* have a desperate need to be loved. Did she?

She knocked on the first door. It slid open. She raised the teapot, her gaze scanning past the four men all raising their beer bottles to her.

Okay, so maybe she might be a smidge thankful for Chet's looming presence only five feet away.

"Chai?" she asked, and they laughed. Then she closed the door on their invitations. Good thing she didn't understand all the nuances of Georgian.

"No Josh?" Chet asked, not looking at her.

"Nyet," she said under her breath.

She went to the next compartment and repeated the offer. This time, four elderly women sat chewing on walnuts. One held out her cup—a glass in a metal housing with an elegant handle—and Mae filled it with an inch of *kepitoke*. The woman would add hot water herself to make tea.

"This could work," Mae said, glancing as Chet as she half closed the compartment door. He didn't comment as she made her way to the next compartment, trying not to jostle the tray. She bypassed the open compartments until Chet alerted her to the return of the conductor. She closed the door, watching as the woman wrestled her large body past Chet, but thankfully, didn't spare her a glance.

Mae waited until the conductor had closed her door, then knocked on the rest of the doors in the car. No Josh.

Chet caught up to her, grabbing her arm as she passed between the cars, nearly knocking the tea onto the tracks. She had no trouble hearing his voice this time, despite the wind. "C'mon, Mae. What if you get caught?"

"Who's going to catch me? The conductors have already checked the compartments and are thrilled to hole up until the next town. This train isn't that long. I can do this."

His grip was locked around her upper arm, and she looked down at his hand.

"Really. I want to get this over with as quickly as you do."

He tightened his mouth into a line. Then he unhanded her.

She moved to the next car.

As expected, the conductor never even looked up as Mae slipped past and began knocking on doors. No Josh, compartment after compartment, car after car. She ran out of tea about halfway through the sixth car, but kept knocking on doors, even after she'd poured her last drop. She simply offered the tea, nodded, and then poured it out, acting surprised when it was empty.

It worked until ten cars down, nearly the end of the train.

She knocked on a door and it opened to four soldiers.

They wore the green camouflage of the Georgian army and looked up at her with interest generated by two bottles of vodka.

"Chai?"

One grabbed his nearly empty glass, still sloshing with the remnants of his beverage. She poured out the empty teapot.

"Zhalka," she said, shaking her head.

But as she shrugged and turned to go, she heard, *"Zehinshina!"*

Uh-oh. The men obviously didn't want the little tea lady to leave.

She acted as if she hadn't heard and started to step away when one of the soldiers, a man who wore the horrors of battle in a scar down his cheek and a leer in his eye, hooked her around the waist and pulled her into the compartment. She dropped the teapot, tripped and nearly knocked her chin on the table covered with empty vodka bottles.

The man wore boots—she got a good look at them just a second before rough hands pulled her up.

She landed hard on the lap of the soldier with the scar.

The man across from her smiled—no, she'd call it a half smirk, half drunken leer—and began to shut the compartment door.

How Chet hated it when his warnings proved right—especially when he knew that the plan wasn't a good idea. And especially when he hadn't tried to stop it before it started. Like the day that David set up the meeting in Kaohsiung harbor, Taiwan, almost two years ago, and Chet had walked into an ambush. His gut prophesied doom—a sour, *this-is-wrong* feeling even as he was placing the weapons in the shipping container. He'd even sensed it the night Carissa slipped into his arms, although then he'd called it something different— shame, or maybe guilt. Now, some twenty years later he knew what to label the feeling.

His own stupidity.

Chet saw the compartment door begin to close, caught a glimpse of Mae's wide, startled eyes, and lunged.

The door slammed on his hand and nearly crossed his eyes with the pain. But he shoved it back—probably harder than he should have because it shook the entire car and the soldiers—no, make that *drunks*—inside. Without a word, he reached for Mae's arm. His other hand, he balled into a fist and connected with the grabber's jaw. And, boy, did it feel good, too. He'd probably added a smidge more oomph into it than he needed. Still, it communicated *sit still and don't move* to the other three as they watched their buddy's head snap back and blood begin to gush from his nose.

By then, Chet had Mae disentangled and was slamming the compartment door behind them.

"Run!" he ordered.

She caught on fast—clearly, her years in the military were kicking in—in fact, if he'd waited, she probably would have delivered a couple of kicks of her own.

Not that it would have made much difference against four healthy, inebriated men.

See, this was what Chet meant by doomed.

He'd intended to push her out the nearest door, but a rod barred it. They'd reached the end of the cars—hence the drunken "security force" barricaded in the last car—so he turned her, using more force than was necessary because she'd clearly figured it out and was already heading back the way they'd come.

At a sprint.

The conductor stood at her door and watched them fly by, confused.

She'd be angry and alerting her fellow conductors in a moment. Perfect.

Chet opened the end door and barreled after Mae into the open place between cars. But as she lunged for the next door, he reached out and stopped her.

Pulled her to his chest.

He was breathing hard. Too hard. She could probably hear his heart pummeling his ribs. "Are you—"

"I'm okay, Chet. I'm okay."

But she held on to him, too—something he attributed to the rush of adrenaline.

She'd nearly been mauled by four men.

But she didn't need protection or anything, right? He held her away from him, arms gripping her shoulders. "How can you be okay? I'm not okay."

She hooked her hands on his wrists, her eyes turning hot. "I'm *fine*."

"Well, just stand there for one more second while I stop myself from going back in there and inciting an international incident."

The train rattled on as he tried to wrestle his heart back to a normal rhythm. Mae's look of frustration soon bled out to concern.

"Chet, I'm really sorry. I didn't think that would happen."

"Well, it did. And…" He shook his head, turning away from her, gripping the rail. "Nothing, never mind." Because what he wanted to say—something along the lines of, *Don't ever do anything like that again,* or, *See, this is why being with you frightens the breath out of me*—would only make things worse.

"Josh isn't here," she said, looking up at him. "He's not on the train."

He lifted his head, meeting her eyes. They glistened, despite the set of her jaw.

"No, he's not."

"Which means what? That he never got on the train?"

He sensed another alternative forming in the back of her mind: Akif had already found them.

Mae pursed her lips. Over her shoulder, through the window, barreling down the aisle toward them, Chet glimpsed the four drunks. The first one held a bloody towel to his face.

"We need to get off the train." Chet caught her hand. "Now!"

"Now? You mean...*now?*"

"Now!"

And then, because all his nightmares had decided to gang up on him at once, he leaped from the train, pulling Mae with him.

He had to give her credit for not screaming as they launched out into space. He'd managed to yank them off the train just as they approached a bridge, one that stretched over a span he didn't dare look at.

They landed hard in a smattering of brush, rock and grasses, tumbling away from the rails, first Chet, then Mae, half on top of him.

They skidded together into a ravine, legs and arms scraping rock and brush and dirt. At some point Mae jerked out of his arms, tumbling away from him. "Mae!"

His head spun as he lay there assessing, even as he searched the ground with his hands for Mae.

"Mae?" He sat up, his head woozy. On the bank above them, the end of the train snaked by, and beyond that, the sky darkened, night closing in.

They needed to get on their feet and back to the village, pronto. "Mae?"

"Over here." Pain laced her voice, and he feared the worst. But she'd pushed herself to a sitting position and was running her hands over her arms and legs. "I think I'm in one piece."

Shouting punched through the rumble of the train. Chet spotted the men leaning over the back of the open car, fists pumping the air, pointing.

Chet couldn't resist lifting a hand to wave.

"What are you doing, trying to egg them on?" Mae stood, glanced over her shoulder and delivered a sour look. "You're about ten years old, aren't you?"

He grinned at her. "Sometimes."

But she didn't grin back. She just limped past him, up the bank, her palm pressing her hip.

"Are you really okay?"

She didn't answer.

"Mae?" She wasn't hurt, was she? Or bleeding? Or maybe she had a head injury? "Mae!"

She stopped and he scrambled up to her, his bruised muscles betraying his age. No more jumping from trains.

She still didn't acknowledge him, even when he put his hand on her shoulder, and turned her to face him.

She looked down at his feet.

"What's the matter?" He thumbed her chin up.

Oh, no, she was crying. Or trying not to, but grimy trails betrayed the truth. Then her shoulders began to shake and she cupped her hands over her face, racking her entire body.

He stood there like an idiot, watching her crumple, afraid to touch her, not sure where to start.

"Are you hurt?"

She didn't respond—just sank down onto the ground, pulled her knees up, and hid her face.

He figured out enough to sit beside her. He debated a moment, then curled his arm around her shoulder. To his relief, she let him ease her toward himself and wrap the other arm around her. "What's the matter?" he said into her hair.

She shook her head.

So he held her, every sob chipping off the frustration he'd built watching her put herself in danger. Maybe she did do impulsive things. But she paid for them, too. "Shh..."

"We're never going to find him." She said it so softly that he nearly didn't hear her. She cleared her throat and sighed the grief from her body. "He's lost. I thought I could just come here, find him, talk some sense into him. What was I thinking?"

She lifted her eyes heavenward, as if including more than just him in the conversation. "We're out here in the middle of nowhere—no car, no money—and Josh is probably already... Oh, God, please don't let Bashim kill him..." She drove her fingers through her tangled hair. "I don't know what I'm doing wrong. I keep trying to untangle myself, trying to get clear of my stupid mistakes, but they follow me, and now Josh is going to get hurt—"

"Mae, the fact that we can't find Josh is not some sort of divine punishment for your mistakes."

"Then why is this so hard?" She turned to Chet, eyes burning, even in the dusk. "It's not like I don't have faith—I have truckloads of faith. I try to live each day by doing what's right. I do everything

I'm supposed to. I help my sister, and I support my mom, and I'm a good friend—"

"You're a *great* friend." He brushed the hair from her face.

"Yeah, so great that I lost my career and my boyfriend. What is living in God's grace if it doesn't mean life is easier, that God is on my side?"

"I don't know, Mae. I think living in grace is more than just hoping for it. I think it's about grabbing hold, not letting go."

He ran a thumb over her cheekbone. "And we hold on for our blessing. Maybe that's what grace is."

"I don't know, Chet. I thought grace was supposed to make you stronger. I can't even do this one thing for my sister."

"For crying in the sink, Mae, you are in a foreign country, trying to track down your nephew who's just run away with a warlord's daughter. In fact, you're so incredibly capable of doing this, it scares me. I admit to being a little bit freaked out, and not just a little ashamed that you're always one step ahead of me."

"I wasn't ahead of you on the train," she said, still not looking at him, in a voice that could tear him in half.

"So you needed me," he said softly, lifting her chin, searching her eyes. "It's about time."

The hope in her eyes was so tender it nearly broke his heart. "I do need you, Chet. I do need you."

And of course, those words coming out of her mouth as she sat swaddled in his arms, the sun backlighting the sky, her beautiful green eyes fixed on his…he traced his gaze around her face and stopped there, at her incredible mouth.

What was a guy to do? He kissed her. Sweetly, touching his mouth to hers, testing, then tasting her tears. She didn't move toward him, but she lifted her face, and he slid his hand around the back of her neck, deepening his kiss ever so slowly. Something about her surrender made him want to weep. Tough, beautiful Mae, needing him…oh, *Mae.* He took his time exploring her mouth, then broke away to kiss her cheekbones, her forehead, her eyelids, then, finally, *finally,* back to her lips.

She sighed in his arms, a slow shudder that seemed to release something she'd been holding tight, and when he broke the kiss, touching his forehead to hers, she looked at him and smiled.

Smiled.

He traced her lips with his finger. "I need you, too, babe."

The train's hum had long since died, taking with it the last of the sun's hold on the day. They sat, swathed in the twilight without words. The wind—warmer than last night's—sifted through the trees, brush and grass around them, and if he wasn't mistaken, he smelled water.

Maybe they'd make it. And not just out of Georgia, with Josh, but really make it.

All the way to happily-ever-after.

NINE

Mae had truly entered a foreign country. And she didn't mean Georgia, with its craggy boulders and cliffs scored only by the silvery track of rail illuminated by the the moon. She ran her hands over her arms, her skin chilled by the wind slithering across the grasses. Her stomach growled, but that moan held no comparison to her heart.

With his kiss, his gentle touch, Chet had awakened the hunger inside, the one that made her want to lean into his embrace.

She needed some sort of anti-heartbreak capsule to survive being around him, or maybe a parachute to use when her high-flying euphoria nose-dived into reality. Especially when the guy turned on the same charm he'd used back in Seattle that had swept her off her feet for a weeklong, whirlwind romance.

Something about the way her heart settled, her breath releasing in relief when he wrapped her in his embrace, made her feel as if finally she could stop running.

"Are you hungry?" Chet had swung his backpack off his shoulder and now crouched in the middle of the tracks, gripping his flashlight in his teeth as he searched through his supplies. He pulled out a bag of walnuts and handed it to her.

"Thank you." She took the bag and he offered a smile.

"I don't want to be accused of starving you in addition to trying to kill you."

"You were trying to save our lives."

The wind tickled her neck, whistling down her jacket. She shivered. Chet stood and edged closer and put his arm around her. "Do we need to stop and rest?"

She shook her head, but if she hadn't been propelled by the deepening dread that Bashim had gotten to Josh first, Mae would have probably sunk into the dirt, curled into a ball and surrendered to the sleep clawing at her body. "I'm fine."

"You're not fine, but we're going to find him—"

"Tell me about your company. How's it going?" She kept her tone light—no need to pick a fight. Besides, she truly wanted to know. "I know you said earlier that everything was fine, but…"

She gave him a small smile, pouring into it true concern.

"Not great, to be honest. I thought I was starting a company that might really help people—you know, hostage rescue, thwarting terrorism, even finding lost children—"

"Looks to me like you're doing exactly that."

"No, *you're* doing that. I'm hunting down a runaway bride."

"Oh."

"Except now, yes, I'm all in for finding Josh." He slipped his hand into hers and held it. "I promise."

His grip warmed her ice-cold hand. She wove her fingers through his, pocketing the walnuts. "What's wrong with the business?"

"I don't know. I keep getting these assignments where I have to dress like SpongeBob or Captain Hook. I recently made a fetching Snow White."

"You're kidding."

"Oh, no, I'm the fairest in the land."

She laughed. "I'm sure you are. But why the costumes?"

"I keep doing security for these multimillionaires with children. Birthday parties, a bar mitzvah and a graduation party that ended up with me in the pool rescuing an inebriated college student."

"Wow. Good thing you were there."

"Just call me Baywatch."

"You do whatever it takes to get the job done.

People notice that because at the end of the day, that's what matters, Chet."

He squeezed her hand. "Not when it costs me you, Mae."

Oh. *Oh.* "Are you saying—"

"Yes, I've missed you. A lot. I've missed your smile. Your courage. When I'm with you, you… inspire me to be better. I remember the first day I met you. We were at Gracie's party, and you stood up to those kids who were dissing you for losing your job. I wanted to throw every one of them off the balcony. And you simply put them in their place—you can deliver a drop-to-your-knees look when you want to."

She smiled, the words *you inspire me* still ringing in her ears.

"I just had to know you. I had to discover the woman behind that dangerous smile." He stopped, turning her toward him. He twined his finger into her red hair, then lifted his other hand, running his fingertips down her face. "Do you think…I mean, can we…can we try again?"

He had the most amazing eyes—even in the pale light of the moon they shone with a longing that made her lean toward him.

Now this was the Chet Stryker she'd fallen in love with. The man who, after just a week, had embedded himself so deep in her heart she'd never been able to shake free of his hold on her.

Probably never would.

He'd made her believe that he respected her and told her that she wasn't a failure. In his eyes, she'd seen her future.

And that was why it had speared her clear through when he'd told her she couldn't fly for him. The memory made her flinch.

He saw it. "Is it too late for us? Have we gone too far?"

She closed her eyes. She didn't want it to be too late, didn't want it to be about Stryker International, or flying, or even her own crazy fears that he'd walk out of her life.

"It's not too late," she said, more hope than conviction in her voice. She lifted her face, rose to her toes and touched her lips to his. He stayed still for a moment, then he drew in a long breath, wound his hand through her hair and pulled her close, kissing her like he meant it.

Just like he had when he'd kissed her goodbye in Seattle, on Gracie's balcony.

She closed her eyes, twined her arms around his waist and kissed him back, letting herself lean into him. Relaxing. Belonging. Believing.

I need you, Chet. She'd said it, and now the truth wove through her. She needed him. Needed him the way a dancer needed a partner. The way a pilot needed a copilot. They were stronger together than apart.

He pulled away and ran his thumb down her face. "Sorry. We should keep going if we want to get back to the town of Gori—and our transportation—by morning."

She nodded. But when they turned to continue the journey, he put his hand on her elbow, and left it there.

It wasn't too late.

Crazy how her words had elicited something akin to his breath being knocked from his lungs, his heartbeat careening in a wild jig through his chest. It wasn't too late.

And then she'd kissed him. *She'd* kissed *him.* And this time, not out of desperation or grief, not out of fear or dread, but to reach out to him.

To bring him into her life. To trust him again.

It wasn't too late.

Dear Chet,

Your last letter made me weep. I know it must have been written from a place of darkness, because I, too, have stood at the edge of my life, wondering if my best days were behind me. That happens when you give something everything you have, and it backfires on you. But what's ahead of you doesn't have to be blackness.

I remember the first time I visited the Grand Canyon. It's so immense that it feels surreal, like it might be a postcard, or a diorama. However, there is breath that circles out of the canyon, full of life. If you close your eyes, you can feel it beckoning, almost as if it waits for you to spread your arms and dive in.

I don't know how to help you through your rehabilitation. I know it's not the physical exhaustion that defeats you, but something deeper, something that feels like evil will inevitably triumph and all your sacrifices feel fruitless. I promise, they matter. They matter to every woman you've yanked out of the horror of human trafficking. To them, and to me, you're a hero.

But the truth is you don't have to bust down doors or parachute in behind enemy lines to be a hero. Maybe being there, showing up in a person's life, believing in them—that's heroic enough.

You're going to be okay, Chet. And when you are, come back to me. I'll be waiting.

Yours,

Mae

He looked at her in the darkness, her hair teased by the wind, her elbow in his grip. He let go and again found her hand. She wove her fingers through his.

I'll be waiting.

She *had* been waiting. She'd written to him every week, and shown up when he'd finally disentangled himself from his final mission, meeting him in Moscow for her best friend's wedding.

But he still wasn't okay, was he? And being back in Georgia only proved it. He'd hardly taken a full breath since returning and even now, the chain around his neck burned his skin, noosing him to the past.

His hand went to it and he ran the thin metal between his fingers.

Something to remember me by. Carissa's eyes flashed in his mind. Deep brown, a hint of tease, too much rebellion in them for his own good. He'd never forget those eyes, nor the way she'd looked at him when he took her in his arms. Trust. Too much trust.

His grip on Mae's loosened.

I need you, Chet.

And he needed Mae. But he couldn't come back to her, not yet. Not until he broke free of Carissa and the hold she had on his heart.

Or rather, the hold her death had on his future.

How he wanted to close his eyes, dive forward into what he saw in Mae's face. Hope. Trust.

Love.

"Are you okay?"

He looked down at Mae, at the concern in her eyes.

"I think I will be."

"When we find Josh?"

He nodded, brought her hand to his lips and kissed it. "Yup. After we find Josh."

TEN

"Mae, wake up. Mae." His voice in her ear, a whispered tenor, made something warm curl inside her. His lips even brushed her neck, and a tingle went through her entire body. His arms' embrace had kept away the cool bite of night, and she longed to sink back in that warm, sweet, comfortable place…

"Mae, now." And then a nudge, not quite so comfortable, on her back. "We need to go."

Go? No more go, please. But even as she thought it, panic forced open her eyes, and she shoved her hair from her face. Oh, she'd been drooling. Nice.

She tried to get her arms under her, but they felt like ramen noodles, bruised and useless. She flopped over onto her back and stared at the ceiling—or *not* the ceiling, more a jumble of boards through which she made out the hazy gray sky, slightly tinged with pink. She shifted, and straw crinkled underneath her, poking into her neck and pants legs. And then the smell. Earthy.

Oh, that was right. A barn. They'd found a barn about, what, a whole ten minutes ago? It must have been at least a couple of hours, because when they'd stumbled into the structure, the moonlight lit it up like the star over Bethlehem.

Chet looked down at her, concern in those incredible blue eyes. "You okay?"

She vaguely remembered dropping into a pile of hay somewhere near the door. "Where are we?"

"I think we're still about forty miles from Gori."

"We can pick up our car at the station."

"If it hasn't been vandalized."

"You're a ray of sunshine this morning."

"Speaking the truth, baby. Expectations are everything. But we'll cross that bridge later. Right now, I'm your knight in shining armor." He dangled a key on a leather thong from his fingers.

"You got us another car?"

"Maybe not quite a car…"

"But we don't have any money."

His smile dimmed. "Yeah, well, I've got my ways."

"Please tell me you didn't promise them I'd muck out the barn or something."

"I wouldn't do that to you," he said, getting up.

And that was when she noticed.

"Your chain, it's gone."

He met her eyes, but she couldn't pinpoint the look in them. He held her gaze without wavering. "I don't need it anymore. But we do need to get out of here, pronto."

"Say no more." She sat up, ran her hands through her hair—oh, what was the use?—grabbed her bag and pushed to her feet.

Chet caught her before she could wobble back down. "Stay upright, partner." But he had a smile on his face that heated her through to her bones.

Partner.

Yes, maybe.

He slid his hand down, fed it into hers, and turned them toward the back of the barn.

Why had he gotten rid of his chain? But she didn't have time to ask—not when she saw their new, uh, *transportation.* As if it had time-traveled from World War II, a camouflage-painted three-wheeled motorcycle sparkled in the sunlight. Well, two wheels plus a—

"Is that a sidecar?"

"It's built right into the bike. It's called a ranger—it's Russian, and it comes with a searchlight, a jerrican and a shovel." He grinned at her as if he was ten years old and had just opened the greatest present on earth from Santa.

"What's the shovel for—burying my dead body when that flimsy little bucket jostles off and I go flying off into the dust?"

"Oh, c'mon, you're overreacting just a little, aren't you? These babies are made for off-road fun—look at the wheels." He kicked one as if she might not know where they were located. "They're knobby, like dirt bikes. We probably won't even need our Lada."

Oh, how she missed the Lada.

"The farmer traded your necklace for the bike... why?" She went over to it, looked inside, too many decades of dirt caked inside the bucket. And the jerrican—well, if it still held fuel, she'd consider it a miracle from God.

Although the past twelve hours had felt a little like a miracle, what with Chet's hand wrapped around hers, and the feeling of hope she'd lost mid-flight from the train stirring again inside.

He'd kissed her, not once, but twice. And it had felt so achingly, wonderfully perfect to be in his arms, to unload it all. Until last night, she hadn't realized just how much she'd carried. Not just her fears about Josh, but her future and her past, all wound together like a boulder strapped to her back. She'd dropped it all right at Chet's feet, and he didn't flinch. Didn't kick it away. Didn't run. Just held her, as if he'd help carry it.

Then he'd kissed her. More of a caress than a kiss, so tender it nearly made her cry. The second time, however, she could feel longing in his touch.

Chet continued to admire his newest mode of transportation. "The farmer says that…it's not exactly his."

"You mean it's stolen?"

"I was thinking…maybe from local Georgian forces."

"Oh, that's great. Which means that if they see us, we're arrested and deported for sure."

"I'll make sure they don't see us." He opened the gas tank, peering inside. "We'll see how she drives on our way to Gori, then stash it and nose around. I'm going to try to get a signal on my cell phone."

"In Gori?"

"You'd be surprised where you can get a signal in Europe. They're more plugged in than we are in the States."

"Even in the backwoods of the Republic of Georgia?"

"That farmer had a satellite dish. He was watching TV when I knocked on his door."

She considered the bike. "Maybe we should offer up a little prayer."

She was only half serious, but the minute the

words left her mouth, she knew that, yes, that was exactly what they should do. Reach out for grace and hold on for dear life, just like Chet had suggested.

And Chet got it, too. He clasped her hand to his chest. "God *is* on our side, and it's time we asked Him for His blessing."

He pulled her in tight, and began to pray.

"Lord, we're in a little over our heads here..."

She couldn't agree more. She wasn't just over her head in a strange country on a nearly impossible mission, but she was so over her head in love with this man... Oh, boy, she needed to put her mind on the prayer.

"...to help us find Josh. Keep Darya and Josh safe today, wherever they are, and point us in the right direction. Protect us..."

Protect us. She closed her eyes. *Why can't you let people help you?* Chet's words thundered back at her. He'd been right—she didn't like people protecting her, because she didn't want to trust them. People let her down.

And not just her father, or Chet. *God* had let her down.

Except maybe He hadn't. Maybe He'd sent Chet to protect her. To give her a second chance to trust Him.

To give her the future He wanted for her.

I'm thinking that I'm not the only one who hit the eject seat, Mae.

She hadn't even been willing to take a chance, to see what God had for her beyond flying. She'd just walked away. From Chet.

From God.

"…and most of all, help us to hold on to Your grace."

I'm sorry, Lord, for not trusting You. For being angry. Thank You for not letting me go. For hanging on to me, even when I didn't hang on to You. Please, protect us. Bless us.

"Amen," Chet said softly. He pressed a kiss to her forehead.

She smiled up at him. "Amen."

Her gaze tracked to the motorcycle. "Maybe I should drive."

His smile fell, just slightly. "Uh…okay. If you want to…"

"Oh, brother." She slipped out of his arms, dropped her bag inside the sidecar and lowered herself to the seat, the leather crackling under her weight. The movement raked up the odor of oil and dust, and she curled her lip as Chet mounted the bike beside her.

Then he handed her a helmet.

"You're kidding me, right?"

"It came with the deal. I insist."

"You'll push me off a moving train, but now I have to wear a helmet on a motorcycle?"

"If I'd had it last night, you woulda been wearing it. In fact, I think you should just put it on and keep it on. Forever."

"Funny," she said as she strapped it on. It couldn't get much worse, anyway. Her hair was matted to her head, her mouth tasted as if she'd eaten caterpillars for breakfast—which she had once done during survival school in the military—and every part of her body itched. And she hadn't eaten for what seemed like decades.

It only made it worse that the happy-go-lucky fella beside her looked devastating with three days of whiskers, wearing those goofy goggles and grinning down at her as if she might be his door prize.

"I'm hungry. I don't suppose we could stop by the house of our friendly neighborhood motorcycle thief and grab some grub?"

He stood and jump-started the bike, revving the engine. "Nope."

"Why not? I think I could eat my bag."

His smile vanished and his solemn expression made her go numb. "Because, while the farmer was selling me the bike, I watched a little television. I think the embassy might have heard about your little moonlight job on the train as a tea girl. Someone got hold of your passport picture."

"What?"

"Your beautiful mug made *Good Morning, Georgia,* sweetheart."

Eleven unheard messages. Chet stood still in the broad sunlight, just outside the metal fencing of the Gori airport, cell phone held aloft—just in case that helped—listening to Wick's fourth message about exactly what he thought of his boss hightailing it to parts unknown and that he'd better check in—

Delete. Next message.

Vicktor. "I'm not sure where you are, Chet, but if it has something to do with the fact that Mae isn't answering her phone either, then you and I need to talk—"

Wow, how easily Vicktor's guesses ran to Mae. Apparently they knew him better than he thought. Delete.

Two more from Wick, one from Luke telling him he'd deposited Brumegaarden's check—at least his account would have money in it—and one from Artyom, calling to say he'd done a security check on the computer.

Chet also deleted the call from Ole Miss Miller, wanting an update.

His gaze found Mae, crouched on the curb, her

bag slung over her shoulder, eating a *peroshke*. He'd bought them an entire bag, bartering the tools Mae had acquired from the Lada with a street vendor. They'd motored past the now vandalized—missing wheels, shattered front windshield, sheared-off steering wheel—car on their way to the airport, where Chet guessed they'd find cell reception. Now Mae sat polishing off her third deep-fried lamb-filled sandwich and guzzling down an orange drink of unknown composition. He'd finished off his three sandwiches on the way over.

Behind him, just beyond the rusty aerodrome, a small airplane spit to life. He watched it taxi down the weedy, cracked tarmac.

Anyone who could fly a Russian airplane…his gaze went to Mae. She could fly a Russian airplane. She could fly a tin can if it had wings. And fix a car. And jump from a train.

She could even hold it together while he careened over bumpy back roads in an ancient motorcycle. Most of all, she could look cute doing it, especially in her helmet and goggles, which she'd finally decided to wear after five minutes of blinking back dust. Her hair streamed out under her helmet and the way she ducked down, hands gripping the sides of the car, she looked like the Red Baron, or a World War I bomber pilot.

He'd probably caught flies in his teeth, thanks to his silly grin.

Chet had to admit he never thought it would be this…well, maybe *fun* wasn't the right word, considering they were on the lam and maybe even targets, now that Mae had made national news. And they were broke. And still hungry. And bruised from their flying leap off a moving train.

The word might be *exhilarating*. Or perhaps *satisfying*. Maybe even *surprising*. Yes, Mae surprised him. With her easy forgiveness, her friendship, her courage, her stamina. The sweetness that filled her eyes when she smiled at him.

Here he'd thought having her on a mission would only make him lose his edge. Curiously, it seemed to make him sharper. A familiar energy buzzed through him, the kind he used to experience on a mission when he and David could read each other's thoughts, or when he knew something was going right.

For the first time in nearly a year, he felt as if he wasn't wasting his time, that he might be doing something that mattered.

His hand went to his neck. He'd hung on to that chain so long, his bare neck felt naked. Or lighter, somehow. He wasn't sure what had made him freely offer the chain Carissa had given him—he'd simply found it in his hands as he asked the farmer to trade it for a way to freedom with Mae.

Maybe, instead of a memory, Carissa's gift had only chained him to the past. To grief.

Next message. "Chet, it's Gracie. Mae's sister called me and she's frantic with worry."

Oh, no, Mae's former roomie. Of course Mae's sister would have her number. And of course, Gracie would immediately turn to Chet.

Apparently, he had somehow broadcast to everyone he knew that he had never really gotten over the redhead who'd slipped under his skin.

And into his heart.

Where she clearly belonged.

Mae rose, dusting off the back of her grimy cargo pants, and wandered over to a newspaper vendor peddling the latest editions from Tbilisi and Gori. She picked up one of the issues, peering at it. What, now she could read Georgian?

Gracie's voice rose in pitch through the phone. "Apparently, Mae hasn't been in touch with her sister, and she said to tell her—if you know where she is—and I'm now quoting, 'Joshy called, and she told him that Mae is trying to find him, and he said he's going back to camp.'"

Back to camp? Everything inside Chet seized up. Did he mean the mission? Where Akif Bashim threatened to…

He shot another look at Mae. She looked up from the paper and motioned him over.

He couldn't move without losing his signal. He held up his hand as he listened to the rest of Gracie's message. "I hope you get this. I'm really worried, Chet, and tell Mae, if she's with you, that she'd better not be in any trouble. Call me."

She hung up. Chet hit Replay and listened to the time stamp, then the message again. She'd called maybe an hour ago.

So, when did Josh get ahold of his mother? Last night? This morning?

He closed the phone.

Josh was going back to the mission. Which meant...what? Images bulleted through his mind—ones he'd long since shoved into the darkest corners of his brain. Bashim binding his hands behind his back. Bashim motioning to Vladik—who'd been Chet's friend—to slam the butt of his rifle into Chet's jaw. The blinding flash of agony as his jawbone cracked. Dirt mixing with the tinny taste of blood, turning to mud in his mouth. A foot slamming into his gut, doubling him over, another in his back, bruising his kidneys. His own cries as another rifle butt, this time to his shoulder, made him howl.

"Chet?"

He hadn't seen or heard her approach. He gasped as Mae took his hand, her soft touch shocking him out of the grip of memory.

"What is it?"

He took a breath and smiled, pushing the memories back—way, way back. "Nothing. Uh—" he cleared his throat, lifting the phone "—I got a signal."

"I saw that," she said, eyes still wary. "You look like you got bad news. You're all pale, and sweating."

He was sweating? He felt his forehead, and he noted that his hand trembled. She saw it, too, one of her eyebrows raising.

"You're scaring me a little, Chet."

He swallowed, found his voice. "Gracie called. And apparently your sister called her."

"Lissa called Gracie?" She threw her hands up. "I've only been gone two—"

"Four. Four days, Mae. The day you left—an overnight trip to Georgia—two days on the road with me, and then today."

She frowned. "Four days. Wow, it feels like two, but then again, it could be an eternity. Okay, so four days. I would think she'd wait a week before she'd start hounding my friends to put out a BOLO.

Next thing we know, she'll call the president and ask him to send in the army."

Chet would be okay with that. Or even just a small precision team of Special Forces operatives. He pocketed the phone. "That's not why she called."

That snapped Mae out of her rant. "Really? Why did she call?"

"Josh called your sister, maybe last night, maybe this morning. Whenever it was, she told him that you were in the country and he said he's heading back to the mission."

It appeared as if everything caught up with Mae at once—fatigue, hunger, fear. She put a shaky hand to her head, her face draining. She took a couple of swift breaths.

"Maybe you should sit down."

"I'm fine. Yeah, okay, I'll sit." She reached out for him, and he caught her hand, leading her over to the curb. She plunked down, and he resisted the urge to suggest she put her head down between her knees.

Although that might be a good idea for him, too.

"Joshy went back to the mission. Where Bashim will be returning to collect him, if we don't get there ASAP," Mae said in a thin voice.

"Yes. Although maybe Josh isn't there."

"Yet."

"Yet." *Holding on, Lord, I'm just barely holding on here.*

"Maybe this is a good thing. Maybe Josh can apologize, and the girl will go quietly…"

Mae's expression betrayed her waning grip on hope. "This isn't going to end well, is it?"

He took her hand in his. "I think we need to get there as fast as we can."

Instead of leaping to her feet and running to the motorcycle, as she might have done, oh, say, a day ago, she looked up at him, a new expression in her eyes. It almost looked like pain—especially when she put her hand to her mouth.

"What? Now you're scaring *me*."

She opened her mouth, but it seemed she had no words. She turned to her bag and pulled out the paper she'd been reading. He wondered what she'd bartered to purchase it.

"This is today's paper. I can't read the Georgian, but the guy on the front looks…well…" Her face had paled.

His probably matched it. Because on the front page, in ugly, large Georgian type, were the words, *Georgian Rebel Leader Sighted on Train to Khashuri.*

Below that, a grainy, much younger, brasher, more foolish version of himself glared out at all of Georgia like a wanted poster, daring Akif Bashim and his minions to find him.

ELEVEN

"Oh, this is perfect, just perfect."

"Are you talking to me?" Chet's voice cut through her thoughts.

Mae looked up from where she paced in small circles beside the bike. Chet had gone into some sort of safe mode about two seconds after laying eyes on his photo. First he'd grabbed the paper, and regardless of her angry demands, refused to read it to her.

He probably didn't have to. She simply had to read his face, and see how it went from shocked, to resigned, to that tight-jawed fear she'd first seen in Tbilisi.

Yeah, it was bad. Because now Akif wanted not only Josh's head, but Chet's, too. The thought could bring her to her knees.

Worse, Chet was the kind of guy who stayed in the fight, who let his partner shoot him to keep his cover, who didn't let his own needs and wants stand in the way of patriotism, or the greater good of others.

He'd pushed her out of his life and back to the other side of the world when he thought she might be risking her life. She didn't believe a word about him being selfish. She watched his face go stony as he wadded up the paper and shoved it into the trash.

Chet Stryker wasn't about to go quietly into the night. Which meant he'd stick around until the bitter end to rescue Josh, regardless of what it cost him. Or how he had to do it.

No, he'd fight back...till the death.

She could read his practically screaming body language, as he gave her a long look and then strode away back to his satellite signal portal and phoned home.

She harbored no illusions that he'd hog-tie her and bribe some local villager to tote her back to Tbilisi to keep her safe if Josh wasn't waiting for her back in Burmansk. Chet had probably already called Vicktor to meet him and force her on the first plane west.

He *had* been on the phone for quite a while, which was why she didn't hear him approach as she continued on her own private tirade. "He's going to get killed, and—"

"Mae, *are you talking to me?*"

She turned to him. "No, I'm not talking to you. Mostly to fate, or whatever ordained this. Because I really don't want to blame God, but I'm not sure what else to do."

Chet looked away from her, toward the tarmac. "God is still on our side. We need to hang on to that."

Yeah, well, her grip had practically gone numb.

"What are we going to do? How are we going to get Joshy from Bashim?"

His eyes cut back to her, then he sighed, his fingers tightening around the cell phone in his hand. "*We* aren't going to do anything. If Bashim has Josh, then I will take care of it. I'll deal with him."

"How?" Even as she asked it, the question turned to acid in her throat. She saw the truth on his face in the way he flinched, then forced a smile.

"Let me worry about that, Mae."

"No! You're going to trade yourself for Josh! Chet—"

"Let's not get ahead of ourselves. Just be glad I'm forcing you to leave."

"Forcing me?"

He seemed to be shaking now, his eyes shiny as they fixed on her. "Do you have any idea how much I'd like to just put you on that motorcycle and drive full throttle to Tbilisi? Or how much I'd like to storm that aerodrome, hijack a plane, and fly you anywhere but here? Prague, Seattle, the Bermuda triangle—anywhere as long as we're together?"

Then, turning, he closed the distance to the bike and snatched up their helmets.

She stood frozen, trying to process his words, pretty sure speaking would only get her into trouble.

He sighed, staring at the two helmets. "But I can't. I can't do that to you, and I can't do that to my country. I can't do that to myself. Because I know that I'd end up hating me, and *you'd* end up hating me—"

"Chet."

He held out the helmet, not looking at her. "So put on your helmet and pray that I have the courage to do what I gotta do here, Mae."

Silence passed in a beat of dread. Another. Then she took the helmet and slowly strapped it to her head.

She wanted to wedge herself into his arms, to tell him everything would work out—that they'd get Josh and they'd escape and no one would get hurt.

But he rounded on her too quickly for her to manage the lie.

"Here's how this is going to go down," he said, his eyes dark, pinning hers. "And I don't want to hear one argument, not one peep, not a breath of rebellion."

Oh.

"We're going to go to Burmansk, right to the mission. If he is still there, you're going to get Josh and convince him to leave. I don't care how. If it takes you longer than five minutes, I'm going to help. And that won't be pretty, so try hard. Then, you two are going to get on this bike and floor it to Tbilisi. No wandering through the forests on horseback or stopping for tea at Americans' houses. To Tbilisi. There, the CIA will put you on a plane out of the country."

"You were on the phone with the CIA?"

"They owe me."

"What about you?"

He climbed on the bike. "Get on."

"What about you?"

"Get on!"

"No. Chet, no! I'm not going to leave you behind. You're coming with us!" *With me.* "I can't—I won't leave without you!"

Something, perhaps the fact that she was yelling, or maybe the way she grabbed his sleeve, got his attention. He turned, his face raw with emotion.

She saw all of it—anger, frustration, fear, even longing—slash across his face.

"Please come with me, Chet."

He took a breath and revved the engine, considering her for a long time. "Get in."

"Please."

He ground his jaw tight. "I'll try."

I'll try. It wasn't enough, but clearly, it was all he would give, for now. She'd take that. Grabbing the sides of the car, she got in and hunkered down inside.

I'll try.

She clutched the sides of the car with all she had as Chet gunned it onto the road toward Burmansk.

I'll try.

"He hasn't been here." Joyce Warner leaned on her shovel, now covered in ash and dirt, sweat trekking across the brow of her baseball cap, along her chin. The villagers of Burmansk had managed, in the past twenty-four hours, to clear away most of the burned rubble—charred boards, twisted metal bed frames, hollowed box-spring mattresses, their spiral skeletal remains like arms reaching to the afternoon sky.

"I promise, if Darya and Josh returned, I'd know about it." She stepped closer, peering down at Mae in the bucket beside Chet. The ancient transport had lost its appeal over the last four-hour motocross event. Dodging potholes and open ditches was more like an off-road race than regular driving.

"We're running out of time," Joyce continued. "But I changed my mind. When you find Josh, you get out of here, as fast as you can. We'll handle whatever Bashim dishes out." Her voice tightened even as she said it, and she met Chet's eyes. "We're not going to let fear run us out of here."

Mae met the news with a grim expression her face. In fact, she'd said nothing, not a peep, since they'd left Gori.

Clearly, he'd scared her into silence.

"He told his mother he was going back to camp," he said, thinking aloud, looking at Mae. "Maybe he meant…"

Then he heard it—Laura's voice, before she'd branded him an enemy. *He told me my place reminded him of a summer camp he attended when he was a kid.*

"He's going to Laura's," Chet said under his breath.

Mae glanced up at him, her eyes wide. "Yes. Of course."

Hope. He could taste it as he spun out on the bike with Mae beside him. Maybe he wouldn't find himself facedown in the mud, a Kalashnikov grinding into the back of his head—

Wait. Wild hope—especially the way it spiked through him, nearly making his head spin— wouldn't do any of them any good. Most likely, Josh and Darya already lay dead among the smoldering remains of Laura's hovel.

A sort of rabid relief swelled through him as he crested the hill and spotted the friendly yellow house, the only hint of life the spiral of welcome from the coal chimney. Of course, he didn't expect the same from Laura. She hated him. Probably had to do with the fact that he helped start the civil war that cost her husband his life. And caused her disfigurement.

Still, if Josh was here...

Chet stopped the bike in the yard and reached out to help Mae from her seat. She took his hand, holding on a little tighter than he expected.

I'll try.

Maybe, in those words, she'd heard yes. ·

When in fact, he meant, *I'll try not to cost you your life*.

Apparently they were back to editing to suit each other's expectations.

"Laura?" Mae yelled, working off her helmet. "Josh?"

Chet reached for his gun, pulling it from his

back waistband, pressing it flush against his leg. If Akif came through that door...

But it opened a crack to reveal Laura, her blond hair down, in a pair of jeans and a blue blouse under a brown buttoned sweater. She stared at them as if they'd returned from the dead. "You two? They haven't caught you yet?"

Chet glanced at Mae. He stopped Mae from advancing, putting her just a shadow behind him. "Did Darya and Josh come back here?"

Laura, regarding him with cool eyes, stepped out onto the porch. "What would make you think that?"

"He called his mother. He told her he was coming here." Laura stared at him and Chet knew. "Where is he?"

"He's not here." Despite her crisp tone, he read sadness in Laura's gaze. "But Darya is."

Chet tucked his gun back into his belt. "Alone?"

"I just told you that Josh wasn't here."

"Where is he?" Mae stepped around him, her voice shrill.

Laura folded her hands over her chest.

"Oh, let them in, Laura!"

The voice jolted Chet, something in it painfully young, painfully familiar.

And then the door eased open and she stepped

out. Long dark, nearly black hair, a princess face, slender body, arms folded against a formerly white oversize man's shirt tied in the front, and a pair of jeans that hugged her long legs.

Carissa.

No. Not Carissa. Because she had blue eyes. Very blue. Regal, almost. Josh hadn't stood a chance. Now, those beautiful eyes looked him over with unabashed curiosity. "So, you're Chet Stryker. You look just like my mother told me."

He wasn't sure how to interpret her tone—it sounded as if she knew him, or at least knew a great deal about him. He didn't remember any of Akif's wives, and had no idea which one might be the mother of this woman. However, clearly his name had lived in infamy around their campfires. She wasn't afraid of him, he knew that much from the enigmatic smile on her face—so she clearly didn't know his mission, namely to haul her back to the father she wanted to escape.

But that smile, it seemed so…as if he'd seen it only yesterday. He felt a strange, inexplicable warmth stir in his chest.

"And you are?"

"Darya…Bashim."

"The daughter of Akif Bashim."

She gave a short laugh and glanced once at Laura, whose expression never wavered from that hard, sad look. Then she shook her head, still wearing that strange smile.

"No. He's not my father."

Oh, no, did he have the wrong girl? Or did the CIA have the wrong girl? That seemed more accurate. They'd given him bad intel, whether by accident or design. Either way, he didn't have to drag this girl back to Bashim, didn't have to force her into marital slavery. He could, right now, figure out a way to get her and Josh and Mae and yes, maybe even himself, out of this country alive.

And without letting Bashim finish what he'd started.

"You're not his daughter? Then why would Bashim burn down the mission and start an international incident—"

"Because he's angry. I defied him by working at the mission, then running away with an American. It's his worst nightmare. And of course, yes, he does expect me to show up tomorrow to marry Akeem."

"So you did get cold feet." He had moved closer and noted that she wasn't so much petite as lean. And a little angry, judging by the glittering of those blue, icy eyes.

"I was foolish, I admit it. I fell in love. I was hoping… I thought Josh and I could have something."

"So now you're ready to go back to Akif and marry this guy?" He glanced at Laura. "To do what you agreed to?"

Darya looked past him, at the motorcycle, then at Mae, and finally back at Chet, and nodded. "I am. I sent Josh back to the mission to go home." His heart softened for her as her chin trembled. "I'm sorry I caused such trouble."

Mae came to life behind him. "Trouble? Seriously? Do you know what your father will do to Josh if he finds him—and you know, he *is* coming back to Burmansk. And if he doesn't find you there…"

Chet put a hand on her arm. "You sent Josh back to the mission? When?"

Then, Mae got it.

Right about the time Darya got it, too. "He's not there?"

"When did you send him?"

"About two hours ago." She looked at Laura. "Right? Or maybe just an hour, I don't know."

"He wasn't on the road, either," Chet said, examining her expression for the truth. She'd gone pale, and real fear filled her eyes.

Yep, she loved Josh.

"Maybe we missed him," Mae said, her voice leaking panic.

Chet strode back to the bike. Something didn't feel right. And if they showed up without Darya, only to find Akif waiting…

He turned and pitched a helmet to Darya. "Get on."

She caught it coming off the porch. As Mae climbed on the back of the bike—clearly wanting to abdicate her seat—Darya wedged herself into the sidecar.

Chet started the bike as Mae slid her hands around his waist. They left Laura staring after them.

Now he understood Laura's sadness—there could be no happy ending for this fairy tale. A sick feeling of dread coiled in his gut as he drove back to Burmansk.

He kept his eyes peeled for Josh, the coil tightening into a fist by the time they reached the mission.

No Josh.

But something had happened. Chet slowed the bike.

Joyce crouched in front of debris before her sprawled husband, his head in her lap, blood oozing between her fingers as she pressed her hand against his forehead.

In the distance a siren whined.

Chet didn't even turn off the bike. He just launched off it and ran to Joyce. Her husband's eyes had rolled back into his head.

"What happened?" He hunkered down next to her.

Someone shoved a wad of cloth into his grip. He moved Joyce's hand away, pressing the cloth against Phil's open wound. He recognized the work of the blunt end of a Kalashnikov.

"Is this Bashim's doing?"

"He came back for Josh, and Phil—" Joyce pressed her hand against her mouth "—Bashim hit him so hard, he just dropped. Not even a sound."

He'd guessed right. Bashim rarely used his fists—he preferred harder objects.

This was not how it was supposed to play out. He was the one Akif really wanted.

"What happened to Josh?" Mae stood over them, her voice just over a whisper. "Did he take him?"

Joyce nodded. "I'm so sorry."

Mae put her hand on Joyce's shoulder and knelt behind her.

Chet put his ear close to the man's mouth. He heard air traveling without constriction. "His airway seems okay. Bashim only hit him once?"

Joyce looked at him with horror. "Isn't that

enough? He's a monster and he has to be stopped."
Her gaze cut to Mae. "He came here because he
found Josh. He left you a message. He wants a
trade."

"For me. I knew it. I'm sorry. So, so sorry."
Darya stood just behind Mae, her hands over her
mouth.

Chet glanced at her, trying not to want to launch
himself at her to wring her pretty rebellious neck.
But his anger quickly vanished at her horrified
expression. The girl looked ready to crumble.

Joyce's expression hardened. "You shouldn't
have left in the first place."

"I know."

In her arms, Phil stirred.

"Is Bashim coming back?" Chet asked, feeling
for Phil's pulse.

Joyce wiped blood from her husband's face.
"He's not. You're supposed to go to him." She
looked up at him then, her pained expression the
final knot in his gut. "Darya…and you, Chet. He
wants both of you for Josh."

Chet closed his eyes. Of course he did.

He'd expected the protest, the angry tone from
Mae. He'd expected her to be the one who freaked
out, who stalked away, hands wild in the air,
yelling.

Only this yelling wasn't in the right language.

A tribal dialect—one Chet had spent years honing—issued from Darya's mouth as she rained down curses on Akif, and his men, and life and, well, it tumbled out so fast, even Chet couldn't keep up.

But why would Darya care? After all, he'd gotten her half-sister killed. Strange she hadn't mentioned that. Strange she wasn't wildly rejoicing that Chet Stryker, aka Pancho, aka the man who'd started the mess, might finally be getting his just deserts.

She whirled around, and shock of shocks, tears careened down her cheeks, unchecked, hot and angry, as she stalked back to him. "Why did you have to come back here? Don't you know he's been waiting for you? Waiting for the day you would walk back into his sights? And no one is going to swoop in to save you this time. He's not going to let you get away. You could roll in there with an army and he'd die with his hands around your neck."

Chet stared at her, seeing the passion in her blue eyes, hearing the pitch of terror in her voice, and time froze.

Carissa.

In the words of this Svan girl, he heard Carissa's voice, heard her pleading for him to take them, right now, out of the country.

He'd stood there in the sheltered alcove just inside the protected gates of the Gori government seat and denied her. Shook his head. Watched her face tighten, her breath heave in and out, as he chose his duty and his job over escaping Georgia and Akif Bashim's power and protecting the woman he loved.

"I've been afraid of this day ever since my mother died. That you'd come here, and Bashim would find out and he'd kill you. Right before my eyes. Retribution for my having lived."

Her words swiped the breath right out of his chest. "What are you talking about?"

Darya slicked the tears, almost violently, from her face and looked at him with a furious, almost rabid expression. "You are so stupid."

Yes, he knew that. But somehow he had the feeling that she meant something more. "I don't understand, Darya." As he stared at her, something vague and painful began to form slowly in his brain. "I know I'm an idiot for coming back here, but why would Akif want to hurt me, because of you?"

She clamped her hands onto her hips, incredulity on her face. Then she blew out a breath and raised her fists. "You still don't get it!"

The fog in his mind had begun to assemble into an image. Still, he stared at her, unable to speak.

"Akif is my *grandfather.* My mother was Carissa Bashim."

Carissa...

"You, Chet Stryker, are my *father.*"

TWELVE

Mae never really thought that Chet would come around to her way of thinking. He'd been so dead set on sending Darya back to her father—for the good of the country—that Mae had held out little hope he'd change his mind. Not only were the fragments of his guilt littered throughout the country in the form of burned buildings, vengeful terrorists and broken lives, but he believed in sacrificing for the greater good. For peace.

Like Darya, marrying a man for the political position, so she could be a patriot.

As soon as the truth issued from the woman's mouth, Mae knew they were true.

And not just because Darya was practically Chet's spitting image. Yes, Mae couldn't believe it had taken her—or him—this long to figure it out. Darya could be a younger, female version of Chet, the way she stood there, battling her father in a staring contest to end all time. She looked every inch as fierce and courageous and resolute and strong and regal as the man who stared back at her, nearly shaking with fury, or maybe disbelief, as he absorbed the heart-wrenching truth.

Carissa hadn't died that night. No, she'd lived, and she'd gone on to give birth to Chet's amazing, gorgeous daughter who lived her own truth, and had grown into exactly the image of her father.

And Mae knew, too, exactly why he'd fallen for Carissa. Because she'd been his match. Brave. Passionate. Resolved.

Mae realized, as she watched Chet comprehend Darya's words, emotion washing over his face, that never, not for one blinding second, would he let her return to Akif Bashim's camp to be given as chattel to some Iranian prince. Never. *Nyet.* Not happening.

Which effectively meant that they'd switched sides.

Because Mae wasn't leaving this country without Josh, alive.

The only scenario she saw before her now—the only one she knew Chet would remotely consider—would entail him riding in like a sacrificial lamb, in the hopes that his presence might appease the wrath of Akif long enough for Josh to escape.

She could almost see that very plan forming in his head as he reached out for Darya.

She gave him her hand, and he pressed it between his. "You're my daughter?"

She nodded, tears rimming her eyes. She managed a shaky smile. "My mother longed to see this moment."

He couldn't meet her eyes. His voice came out low, carefully enunciated, as if he had trouble finding it. "What happened to her?"

"She died a few years ago. Cancer. We didn't catch it until the end. But she had always hoped we'd meet. That you'd know she lived, and that she hadn't forgotten you."

Her words resounded in Mae, and she hoped Chet heard them, *really* heard them. Carissa hadn't died. He hadn't caused her death.

"You're my daughter," he said, and his voice contained wonder that made Mae want to cry, too. "You're my *daughter.*"

Then he pulled Darya to him and wrapped her in those amazing arms, the ones that could make anyone feel safe, and held on. He buried his face in her neck, and then...

He was crying. Sobs racked his shoulders, even as he reached around to hide his face. But she could hear him huffing.

Finally.

How she wanted to move toward him, to hold him, tell him that yes, it would be okay.

But this moment didn't belong to her.

Still, she wanted to weep with him. To rejoice and cry for all he'd discovered here, in the place he'd wanted to forget.

And then, of course, Chet put his daughter—his *daughter!*—away from him, held her by the shoulders and said the words Mae knew were coming.

"There's no way I'm going to let you go back to Akif, so you might as well drive that thought from your mind, Darya. It's over. You and Mae are leaving. Right now, on that bike, for Tbilisi."

Oh, she was her father's daughter. She shook out of his grip, clearly gearing up for the fight. "Are you kidding me? I'm not leaving so Grandfather can kill you. And Josh. I *love* Josh." Her gaze tracked to Mae. "I do. He's kind and wonderful and brave."

"Then why go back? You know that Akif will only make you marry this Iranian," Chet said, sounding like he'd already won the argument.

Mae wanted to raise her hand and suggest a few answers to that question.

Darya beat her to it. "Because my grandfather will kill Josh if I don't go back. And because I'm just like my parents. I don't care what it costs me to do the right thing. I figured that out when Josh and I got to the train station. I'm just sorry it took that long." She glanced down at Phil.

His eyes were open, his hand pressed to his wound, looking at all of them as if they might be some sort of terrible train wreck.

Yeah, well, it was only going to get worse.

"You're not going, Darya." Chet sounded more like a father every second. Or maybe unyielding and bossy was his default mode.

"Chet," Mae started, and he looked at her as if seeing her for the first time in years. "Maybe you should listen to her."

She knew he was struggling to respond because a tiny knot formed at the back of his jaw.

Mae kept her voice calm. "I'm just saying that if we all stop and think, maybe we'll find a solution. A plan that keeps everyone alive." *Because I don't want you to die, either.* With everything inside her, she tried to put that message into her eyes.

But whatever hope they'd had of holding on to grace, of finding that blessing, of seeing the future together, died when he shook his head, walked over to the motorcycle and started the engine.

Then, without a backward look, as Darya ran after him screaming, and as Mae stood stock-still, everything inside her thrumming with pain, he drove away.

Darya turned into a figure of despair as she wrapped her arms around her waist and dropped to her knees in the dirt. Then she lifted her head and let out a wail that ripped through Mae.

Mae sank down behind her and pulled her into her arms.

"We'll get him back," she said softly, lying with everything inside her.

Chet swerved to miss a pothole and managed to rocket the bike over a speed bump that sent it flying. It slammed with a puff of dirt back on the road. Okay, slow down.

Think.

He would admit to impulsively jumping on his bike and driving away before either of the women he loved—and yes, he *loved* Darya—could put their lives in danger.

The minute Darya had said, *"You're my father,"* he'd experienced an explosion inside that consumed the pain and self-hatred, and revealed one body-shaking truth.

He hadn't killed Carissa.

And right after that came the gift. He had a daughter. A beautiful, smart, amazing daughter.

He let that settle for just a moment before he went to...

Who wanted to sacrifice herself. Because she was like her parents.

I don't care what it costs me to do the right thing.

And she would do the right thing. She and Mae together would, because he could read Mae better than she thought, and one glance at her told him that behind those amazing green eyes, she was cooking up a plan.

One that would end with her in a body bag and Darya married to some prince she didn't love so she could spy for the CIA and him gripped in a fist of pain so tight he'd probably never break free.

Nor want to.

So why waste time? He'd jumped on his bike and floored it without a backward look, without a thought as to what he might be doing or how he'd possibly find the courage to face Akif. It was just a full-throttle, emotional reaction.

Perhaps Mae had a point. Impulse might be all he had left.

He'd turned to see the mission obscured behind the hills. Stopping the bike on the road, he took a breath and swiped his hand across his sweaty forehead. Now his heart hammered against his ribs, and despite the wind that kicked up the dust and carried the scent of smoke, he continued to sweat.

Sometimes his jaw still cracked when he opened it. And the odor of antiseptic could awaken his gorge. He'd logged way too much time in sanitized hospitals during his military life, starting right after the medevac flight out of the Republic of Georgia twenty years ago. Thanks, Bashim.

This time, he'd be lucky if he made it *to* a hospital.

Lucky. Blessed, maybe.

Chet crossed his hands over the handlebar of his bike, leaned down. Deep breath. Just start the bike and go. All he had to do was stay alive long enough to help Josh escape.

Then, Josh, Darya and Mae would leave. Even if it killed her, Mae would leave the country with Josh. Despite her impulses, he could count on her priorities.

Please, Mae.

Dear Chet,

I've never been shot, so I don't know what it's like to feel broken as you mentioned in your last letter. I do know what it feels like to have everything you love stripped away, to face emptiness and to call out to God and get only an echo of your own voice back. And in these moments, I have to grab my Bible and assure myself that I'm not alone. That He has my back. Today I read Psalm 68. Did you know that God says that daily He bears our burdens? In other translations, it says He "loaded us with benefits." And that word *benefit*—in the Greek—also means "cradle."

I know you're probably juiced up on painkillers right now, but you're also cradled, Chet. Right in God's arms. He's got you.

The first time I jumped from an airplane, I was eighteen. I was terrified, so I went tandem. But getting up there on that wing and pushing off—suddenly all my fear leaked out of me. Why? Because the expert was right behind me. He had me.

I flew. I flung my arms out and screamed. My only view was the world, spread out like a three-dimensional map below me.

I know you feel alone, Chet. But I'm thinking about you—and God has you.
From the skies,
Mae

He'd kept that letter in his Bible. When this was all over and his pals went to his flat and packed up his belongings, they'd find it right in the passage next to Psalm 68. He had actually underlined the last part—"Our God is a God who saves; from the Sovereign Lord comes escape from death."

Escape from death. Probably David meant spiritual death…only, he *was* a warrior, so, no, maybe he had meant physical death. Painful, bloody, ago-nizing death.

Escape from death.

"God, I'm holding on here, with everything I've got. Please, please help me not to let go."

Chet didn't have to dig deep to remember the landmarks that led him north, deeper into the oak and poplar forests, through the little village where he'd spent that last night with Carissa and right into the crease where Bashim niched his camp, deep in the foothills of South Ossetia. Darkness pooled in the crannies of the giant ridge he followed, the dirt one-lane road easily defensible from the pockets inside jagged boulders stacked on the hillside. The breath of the gathering winter cut like a knife as it chapped his face.

Night had nearly fallen by the time he pulled into Bashim's camp. Chet felt eyes tracking him as a finger of icy sweat rolled down his spine. When he got close, two soldiers, wearing ragged sweaters and bearing black M13s, eased out from behind a very impressive, and probably stolen, Russian tank.

The guards motioned him beyond their post and lifted radios to their mouths.

Bashim had upgraded his technology in the past twenty years.

Chet noted more upgrades in the mesh camouflage

fencing that encircled the camp, the row of transport trucks, the ten-year-olds holding AK-47s, watching him with dangerous eyes as he pulled up.

Bashim clearly no longer feared detection. Where once he'd hidden his camp—composed mostly of cinder-block shacks with a pot for plumbing—under expansive oaks and bushy poplars, now it sat in the open with long barracks, still of the cinder block variety, and probably still with questionable plumbing. The heavily fortified camp didn't seem in the least intimidated by the flimsy threat of Georgian—or any other—troops.

Especially not a lone man on a jalopy motorcycle.

The kids nearly laughed at him as they motioned him through the gate, no more than a few two-by-fours nailed together. Another dig at the Republic. Apparently, they didn't need security when they owned the hearts and minds of the youth.

Chet didn't have to wait for a welcoming committee. As soon as the gate closed behind him, he saw an envoy of soldiers. Or mercenaries. Or freedom fighters. Whatever they were calling themselves these days.

The kind he'd probably armed himself so long ago.

He recognized a couple of older thugs. He couldn't call up their names, but their dark, empty eyes bored through him with bone-chilling familiarity. Clearly, they remembered *him*.

He stepped off the bike. Held up his hands in surrender.

The voice he dreaded came from behind him, like a bullet between the shoulder blades. "Welcome back, Pancho."

THIRTEEN

Of course Chet had walked out of her life. Because that was what men did around Mae. Maybe they didn't always hop on the back of a motorcycle out of *The Great Escape* but still, in the end, they always left her standing in the dust, blinking back gritty tears.

Not that she blamed him, really. Because frankly, Mae might have done the same thing, instead of wasting her breath fighting with an immovable force. Darya so closely resembled her father in spirit that Mae thought she might be watching Chet fume as Darya stalked the front room of Joyce and Phil's tiny three-room house. It was built like every other house in the village, with a main room, galley kitchen and one back bedroom. They'd obviously opted to live like the locals instead of building an Americanized home in the Georgian backcountry.

"I can't believe he just…left!" She rounded on Mae, fire in those breathtaking eyes. "Just

ignored everything I said, hopped on the bike…
and left!"

Mae couldn't even respond to Darya's words.
She just stood there, a crushing burn in her chest,
remembering Chet's arms around her, remembering…trusting him.

He'd driven away without a backward glance.

Her jaw tightened as she looked at Darya. "I
think he didn't know what else to do. He acted on
instinct to protect the…" she let herself hear her
words "…people he loves."

The people he loves. Darya, and her. Because
he knew that Mae was just as likely to hop on
the bike and full-throttle it to camp after Josh.
Reckless, he'd called it. He might rename it now.
Desperate.

Still, she knew—just *knew*—this would happen.
Maybe not here, or now, but someday. She'd hand
her heart over to some man again, and he'd walk
away.

While she did nothing to stop him.

Not that she had any time to think with his,
well, she'd say it—impulsiveness. But she hadn't
screamed or run after him. She'd just silently let
him go. Just like the day her father left. She'd
stood there, words lodged in the back of her throat,
watching her life dissolve before her eyes. She
hadn't even made a peep.

Maybe that was why she jumped at the first sign of trouble, and longed for people to need her. Because if they walked out of her life, she wasn't going to drag them back.

She *had* panicked when Chet rejected her in Moscow and had nearly bolted out of his life. She'd turned and fled, and she wouldn't even have heard him calling her back. If he had.

Why does it scare you so much to rely on me?

She had to do more than just trust him. Maybe she had to really hold on to him. Fight for him.

Maybe it was time to stop standing on the doorstep in the rain.

"We have to get him out of there," Darya said.

"I know." Mae watched Darya as she stalked the perimeter of the room. This woman radiated frustration. And Mae could practically hear the gears turning in her mind.

She wasn't the only one trying out scenarios.

"Can we get into that camp?"

Darya's head snapped up. "I could."

Mae folded her arms against a spurt of hope so vivid she knew it was wrong. She owed it to Chet to protect his daughter.

Because she knew that he'd be protecting Josh. Josh would see Chet, and would know that Mae hadn't given up hope.

"Is there any chance your grandfather will release Josh?"

Darya shook her head. "My grandfather needs weapons. I'm his ticket to a huge dowry. He's not going to let that get away." She said it without flinching, without any tone that might reflect repulsion, although Mae could hardly hear the words without wincing. Darya must have read her expression. She lifted a shoulder. "It's the way here. And I knew that. I should have never..." She turned away. "I'm such an idiot. Josh is going to get killed, and it'll be all my fault."

Oh, Mae recognized that, too. Yes, this girl certainly was her father's daughter, blaming herself for the choices of others.

"Listen, Darya, it's not your fault. Sure, you asked him for help, but he could have said no. I know Josh. He wanted to help you, or he wouldn't have done it, I promise you that. Josh helped you because he loves you, and you need to let him take responsibility for it."

Darya stared at her as if testing her words. "I just can't get past the fact that I caused this. And that now, everyone is paying for it. Josh and Phil—and now my father."

"You know, that's a lot of burden to bear for one young woman." Joyce stood at the threshold to the bedroom, arms crossed in front of her. "And I'm not sure that all of it belongs to you, anyway."

Darya rounded on her, her voice tight. "Are you insinuating that Josh is to blame for my grandfather torching your property and—"

"I'm saying that regardless of your choices, God says that He will bear your burdens."

Darya narrowed her eyes at her. But Joyce's words found Mae, and rattled through her. Yes, God *had* said that. She'd written nearly those very words to Chet over a year ago. God daily bears our burdens.

"Why would God bear *my* burdens?" Darya said, almost icily.

Joyce stepped toward her, her voice gentle. "Because He wants to. He's on our side, despite our foolishness. We're the ones who expect ourselves not to make mistakes. Why do you automatically assume that God is your accuser? Can't He be your champion?"

Darya held Joyce's gaze a long time before she turned away, stalking out the door.

But Mae stood, unable to move. She did live life as if God was always frowning at her. She'd developed a posture of ducking.

At least since she'd walked away from the career He'd given her.

But maybe…maybe He hadn't left her. Maybe

He kept tapping her on the shoulder, reminding her that He was on her side. Despite her impulsiveness and especially her fears.

Oh, she hoped so.

Joyce's attention turned to her as she gave Mae a tight-lipped sigh. "I don't know what it'll take to get through to her. But even in this, God hasn't abandoned us. We just need to hold on to His grace, and trust Him to save us."

Hold on to His grace. Hold on to her champion.

Mae nodded as Joyce returned to the bedroom to check on Phil, closing the door behind her with a soft click.

Darya stood on the front porch, arms folded, as if trying to keep herself from shattering.

Oh, how well Mae knew that pose. Closed. Alone. Clinging to yourself for strength. She went over and took Darya's hand. "Darya."

Darya sighed but didn't pull away. "Listen. I hear you. Josh makes his own choices. But so do I. And I'm not going to let my grandfather kill him or my father. Not if I can stop it."

"You can't go back there."

Darya met Mae's eyes, a familiar determination in them. "I'm not afraid to marry Akeem. I know him. We met in London. He might even love me.

And I am fond of him. It's not what you and my father think."

Sure it wasn't. Mae stopped just short of rolling her eyes. "Your father would kill me if I let you go back. We have to find another—"

"There is no other way!" Darya's voice flared. She cut it back to low. "I promise you, no one can get into his camp. My grandfather is in charge of half the army of South Ossetia, and the other half are afraid of him. The last person who tried to cross him was beaten until he bled from his ears, tied up in the center of camp and left there to die. No water, no food and…" The memory flashed through Darya's eyes. "That's why I ran. Not because I have to marry a man I hardly know, but because the man he killed was only nineteen. He was a friend. And I knew without a doubt that my grandfather would do the same to Josh, or my father, or anyone that got in his way. He's an evil man. And I was scared. I knew that if he discovered…" She put a hand to her mouth.

"That you were going to betray him, he'd do the same to you?"

"The same thing he did to my mother." She looked at the floor. "She nearly died after he let his men beat her."

"But she stayed with him," Mae said.

Darya said nothing. When she looked up, she

wore a rueful smile. "Yes, she did. How do you think the CIA knew of his whereabouts all these years?"

Clearly, patriotism ran thick in her blood. She'd inherited it from both parents.

Mae shook her head. "Then letting you return is a huge mistake. If Bashim won't even spare his own daughter, and Chet is there… Well, if your grandfather even breathes wrong near you, Chet will lose it. And then…" Nope, Mae couldn't go there.

Reckless. Impulsive. Yeah, she had some hard-truth words for him, too.

Once she got him out of there. Because she wasn't going to let another man walk out of her life.

"I have to go back. Because I have to finish what I started."

Mae met her hard-eyed gaze with one of her own and nodded. "Me, too, Darya. Me, too."

"Dude, you don't look so hot."

Oh, please, he didn't want to wake yet. Like tentacles, consciousness wrapped around him, yanked him forward, into the cold wash of pain. And this wasn't over—not nearly, if he read Akif Bashim's broken-toothed yellow smile correctly. Bashim had welcomed him by spitting in his face.

He'd aged in his eyes more than anything—they'd blackened, like those of a snake, and white laced his graying beard. But he'd also grown a paunch, like a good dictator, and his pudgy hands lacked the power Chet remembered when he delivered the first head-jarring blow into Chet's cheekbone.

No, Chet wasn't prepared to drift back to the living, not when the only thing that awaited him was more of Akif's men—and their fists—reminding him of his mistakes.

Like not telling Mae before he left that he loved her. Sure, he'd said he was sorry and told her that he needed her, but had he mentioned that being with her these past few days had made him realize exactly how lucky he'd been to have her in his life? Yeah, it opened all the old wounds, but he'd glimpsed, like a blind man seeing for the first time, just how good—no, great—they were together. How wrong he'd been to think that being around her would make him less keen-minded, less able to do his job.

Being with her reminded him of everything he had to live for—and sacrifice for.

So he lay there, the floor cool against the burning pain throughout body, and refused to open his eyes.

Not that he could anyway. His eyelids felt sticky, and fat. And his jaw had reloosened. At least one tooth—yep, that was a molar—moved beneath his swollen tongue. He groaned, and the voice that had called him back to consciousness sounded too eager when it said, "I can't believe you're alive."

"Me either," he said, more of a moan than words. But just to make sure, Chet opened his eyes as best he could. And yep, he was right back in the too-vivid past, lying in a cell in Akif's prison, the only fresh air filtering in from a small, gridded window high in the wall through which a meager slant of bloody light told him the sun had abandoned the day. It shone just enough for Chet to make out the chipped cement floor, a solid metal door on unbreakable hinges, and a broad-shouldered, tight-jawed young man with enough auburn in his hair and concern in his eyes for Chet to peg him as Josh Lund.

"Let me help you," Josh said, as he anchored his arm around Chet's shoulder and pulled him up to a sitting position.

Chet's head spun and he wanted to slip back into oblivion. But he blinked past the thunder rolling around in his head and attempted to assess his injuries. And their chances of survival.

"How long have I been out?" His voice slurred through his fattened lip.

Josh reached back, grabbed a rag in a bucket of

water, wrung it out, and handed it to Chet. "Your nose is bleeding."

He pressed the cloth to his nose. The pain that speared into his head confirmed that his nose had been broken—again. Well, he'd never been a beauty queen.

"So who are you and what did you do to make them angry?" Josh moved away, nearly out of the light.

"You first. What's your name? What are you doing here?" Chet asked, just in case he wasn't the redheaded nephew of the woman he loved.

He had a fuzzy spattering of dark whiskers and wore a pair of dirty jeans and an equally grimy Arizona Wildcats sweatshirt. "My name's Josh and I, uh…" Josh ran a trembling hand down his face, despite the tone of bravado in his voice. He was clearly scared to death, but not willing to show it. So much like Mae, it was freaky.

"I had a friend who needed help. I got in a little over my head."

"What kind of friend?" Chet asked, feeling suddenly like a curious, well, father who was talking to the young man who loved his daughter.

Daughter. He still couldn't think the word without feeling a rush of sweet, fresh air in his soul. Carissa and he had a daughter.

"A beautiful, smart, brave friend whom I didn't

deserve. And only really figured that out about an hour after I got here. She tried to protect me. She's probably still trying to figure out a way to protect me, to get me out of here. Only—" he blew out a long breath "—I'm really hoping that my aunt finds her first and talks her out of it."

Yeah, him, too.

"What's your full name, son?"

"Josh Lund." He peered at Chet through the last fragments of light. "I have to admit, you look worse than my aunt's picture of you." Then he grinned.

Oh.

"Although after what you did to her, I shouldn't be feeling so sorry for you right now." Josh's smile vanished. "She was pretty broken up about you."

"For the record, I made some big mistakes. But I love her, Josh, and I wish I hadn't let her go."

Chet wasn't sure why, but saying that aloud gave it power and stripped the last of the clinging fear right out of him.

He loved Mae. And if he got Josh out of here, the kid would live to tell her. She'd know that Chet hadn't walked out of her life. Not willingly.

That seemed to satisfy Josh. He got up and stared out the window. "My mom said Aunt Mae was coming to Georgia. Is she okay?"

"Last time I saw her, yes." He didn't want to let

his mind travel beyond that to the fact that Mae and Darya were probably plotting to rescue them right now.

How he wished he had the power to order Mae to take his daughter and run.

You don't respect me, she'd said to him.

No, that wasn't it. In fact, if anyone had the brains and the courage to launch a full assault on Akif and his band of terrorists, it would be Mae.

No, he respected her. But she terrified him.

"How'd you get pulled into this?"

Chet looked at his knuckles. He'd thrown a couple of licks back. Probably wasn't the best choice, but it had felt good at the time.

"Mae called me."

"She called you? She told me she was never going to talk to you again."

"I came for Darya. To find her and bring her back to camp so she could marry...the..."

Josh stared at him with a look that made Chet wonder if his next beating would be coming from the kid across the cell. He held up a hand. "I changed my mind. I know it was the wrong thing to do."

Josh narrowed his eyes, as if still trying to decide whether to re-bloody his nose. "And what changed your mind?"

He looked at Josh. "Darya."

Josh braced a hand against the side of the cell and sighed. "Yeah. She can do that. She has a way of looking at you that makes you forget your own name. Or at least your priorities. And then she makes you wonder if you might be some sort of superhero. I don't know what got into me but I know it was right to help her. And I'll always believe that, regardless of what happens."

Josh smiled at Chet, and he recognized in the young man everything that made Mae who she was—brains, courage and devotion. The belief that giving up her life for others was the right thing to do. He'd been wrong—her actions didn't come from desperation, but rather a love that went beyond herself.

Regardless of what it cost her.

She deserved to be loved back the same way. Which meant letting her live her life, with challenges and risks, and rewards and joys whether she wanted to pilot a plane or jump right on out of it.

Josh turned to the window. "So, why are they so angry with you?"

"Because maybe I started a bit of this trouble when I armed them for war twenty years ago. But I think the kicker came when I fell in love with Akif's daughter." He raised an eyebrow at Josh when the boy turned.

If he wasn't mistaken, the kid paled slightly,

swallowing hard. His voice emerged a tone higher when he said, "Really?"

"Yep."

Josh blew out a breath and seemed to steel himself. "I guess I'm next, then."

"Maybe. But not from Akif, Josh."

"I don't—"

"Akif isn't Darya's father." He smiled. "I am."

Josh stared at him, blinking, his mouth cracking open and closed.

Yes, kid, you absconded with my daughter. And you had better not have—

"I promise, sir, I took very good care of her…"

"Now it's sir, huh? Calm down. I just found out. And Mae is your biggest advocate. She vouched for you more than a few times."

Josh said nothing, just stared out the window. "They're not going to let us go, are they?"

Chet leaned back against the cold wall, feeling every blow, every kick, every bruise embedded in his bones. But, strangely, now that he was facing Akif again, the old guilt had loosened inside him. Maybe turning to God, holding on with both hands to His grace, had made him release his grip on his regrets. On the broken, bloody shards of his life that he'd thought he'd never escape.

And the fears that he thought he could never let go of.

"Kid, I'm pretty sure the fight's not over yet." Chet grimaced. "I'm not quite ready to let them win. Are you?"

Josh turned, a defiant look in his eyes and a game smile. Ah, see, there was the Lund gene he knew so well. "Nope, not quite yet."

"Chet Stryker, international securities," Chet said, holding out his hand.

Josh met it. "Josh Lund, international troublemakers. I think I'm just the junior member, though."

Chet smiled. "Yes, son, I believe you are."

The last of the sun winked out as a new sound rumbled into the room. It started as a dull rhythm and soon grew to a roar just beyond the building.

"What is it?" Josh peered out into the blackness.

"Sounds like a helicopter."

Josh slid down into a crouch. "Oh, no. I think it's Darya's fiancé, Akeem Al-Jabar." His voice was muffled, as if he'd covered his face with his hands when he said, "I think our time is up."

FOURTEEN

Oh, this couldn't be good. Mae trained her field glasses on the chopper—a Russian-made Mi-17—as it cleared the mountain ridge then set down in the darkness of Bashim's camp. Maybe, if she could get her hands on it…

"That's Akeem," Darya said softly beside her. "He's early, by two days."

Nope, definitely not good.

They lay hunkered down on a ridge opposite the camp. Darya had pointed out the prison, and they'd outlined a rough, if not nearly impossible, plan for Darya to surrender to her grandfather and then open a back gate for Mae to slip through and release Josh. And Chet, if he was still alive.

They'd watched in silence as the guards dragged Chet—and *dragged* might be an impotent word for the way they yanked and threw his body across the yard and to the prison. Which meant the prequel couldn't have been pretty. *Please, God, don't let him die.*

Darya wore a traditional hijab, along with her jeans and a clean blouse Joyce had lent her. Better to look as non-Western as she could as she offered herself in sacrifice to her grandfather's schemes. And to the CIA.

Mae couldn't believe that she had consented to this crazy plot. But if she hadn't, without a doubt, Darya would have gone in alone, her only strategy the impulse of the moment. At least with Mae, she had a plan.

And the first step was to make her grandfather believe that she would marry Al-Jabar. Not that Mae would let her stick around to go through with it—she didn't care what kind of world-peace game the CIA was playing.

"Is it too late?" Mae trained her eyes on the chopper, but she couldn't make out anything except the flood of lights that lit up the entrance of the camp like a Broadway show, spotlighting Darya's brilliant return.

Her gut started to churn.

"I think if I leave now, I can negotiate Josh's release."

"And Chet's?"

Darya pulled the hijab over her face and stood up. "I'm leaving him in your hands. Don't let me down."

Her life motto—never let your friends down. Mae nodded.

"I'll give you a signal when the back gate is open. The floodlights will flicker. I'll be watching for you near the prison doors, and when I see you, I'll distract the guards."

And Mae would find Chet.

"Hopefully, my grandfather will have already released Josh."

And hopefully, Chet would still be alive.

"Then we'll hop in one of those transports and try to outrun them." She glanced at Mae. "It's a good plan."

Yeah, if they were Rambo and the Terminator, sure.

"Absolutely," Mae said. "It'll work."

Clearly they were both lying through their teeth, but there was no way Mae wanted to tell Darya that the only ones who had a good chance at living through this were Darya and Josh.

Mae prayed for that much, at the very least.

To her surprise, Darya reached out and touched Mae's arm. "We'll finish this, Mae."

Something about Darya's words gave her hope, even as she watched the figure slip into the night, down the cliff.

Yes, they would finish this, and then Mae would tell Chet that she didn't care—well, she did, but she'd try *not* to care—that she wasn't flying for him. That she just wanted them to be together, that life was a trade-off sometimes, and that she wanted to make room for him in her world. Even if she had to sacrifice something she loved.

She loved Chet more than she loved flying.

Behind her, she heard footsteps, the crunch of grass—

She turned, the field glasses in her hand already swinging. But her assailant caught them with one hand, pressing his other hand over her mouth.

"Shh!"

Mae brought her knee up, hard. The breath whiffed out of the man above her. She slammed her elbow to his face. He recoiled with a grunt, letting go of the glasses.

It gave her enough room to lean back and bull's-eye her foot in the center of his chest. She shoved him hard and he sprawled back onto the grass. Then two more men appeared.

They'd picked the wrong girl this time. She hit her feet.

"Mae!"

The one holding the black tech-gear bag dropped the sack to the ground and shone a light on himself. Chet's partner, Vicktor Shubnikov. He brought a long finger to his lips, his eyes pinned to her. "Shh. We don't want anyone to catch us."

Ya think?

"Vicktor? What—"

"You're *yelling*."

She shut her mouth and flung her arms around him, right around all that black protective gear and the M-16 he wore over his shoulder. Solid, fierce. He'd come for her, for Josh. "I'm sorry, God, that I doubted."

Vicktor put an arm around her waist and pulled her tight. "I'm not sure I understand all that, but I'm glad to see you, too. We didn't know what to expect when we followed Chet's GPS signal from his cell phone into the hills."

She couldn't even find words. Vicktor had come for them. Former FSB agent turned independent contractor, the guy who had saved Gracie's life twice (no wonder she married him) and the man who would currently be voted Most Likely to Know How to Bust Chet Out. Yes, she might be a smidge glad to see him.

He pulled back and flicked off his light. "You okay?"

She inhaled a long breath and tried to flush the shaking from her body. "Yeah, except who was the thug?" She deliberately glared at her assailant. "You could have said something like, 'friend not foe' or how about even, 'Mae, don't scream. I'm a good guy.'"

"I did shush you." He held out his hand. "Luke Dekker. I'm one of Chet's men."

"'Shh' doesn't quite cut it out here, pal."

"Sorry." In the dark, she could barely make out a wry, apologetic smile. "Next time, I'll be better prepared."

"Let's hope there isn't a next time. I don't like this idea of our fearless leader running off without telling us." A man stepped out from the shadows behind Vicktor. He had a build not unlike Chet, although maybe bulkier. His voice, a baritone, rolled through the night like thunder. "Wick. It's good to finally meet you, Mae."

She remembered Chet talking about him—Wick had been the first person he'd hired, an old pal from his Special Forces days.

"Okay, I tapped into their radio chatter. Apparently the helo is staying the night. And the girl isn't in camp yet," said a Russian accent from the darkness.

"Artyom!" Mae startled the young man, who had come up behind Vicktor. She just barely resisted giving the Russian techie a one-armed hug. "Who else is here?"

"Believe me, Gracie tried to get on the plane. But she's manning the office. And David and Yanna were worried, but with Yanna still working for the KGB, it wouldn't work for David to come cruising down here. They did, however, grease the skids for us to get here. And Roman and Sarai are still in far eastern Russia. He's working undercover somewhere."

Of course he was. With the Russian mafia going global, Roman could be working anywhere as a Cobra operative.

"How'd you get here so fast?" She still couldn't believe that Vicktor stood before her. She traced his face, despite the swell of darkness. Lean, with a squared chin, blue eyes that always seemed so serious. Of course he was here in the back hills of the Republic of Georgia. Where else would he be when his partner was in trouble?

"Actually, we were already in Georgia when we picked up Chet's signal this morning. We didn't have to do calculus to figure out that you were in trouble when Chet abandoned ship—"

"You automatically assumed I was in trouble?" Okay, that irked her. Mostly because it hadn't been her getting into trouble on all those rescue missions. Well, not entirely.

Vicktor smiled, apparently egging her on. "No, I automatically assumed that if you were in trouble, Chet would be there."

Oh.

"And, of course, knowing his history in Georgia,

the team got worried. We just wanted to make sure—"

"He got out alive."

Every man in the group had geared up in black, including Artyom. Yes, they'd come to make sure Chet got out alive…and maybe even more, if things got ugly.

"Is Chet down there?" Vicktor took the field glasses from her hand.

"He's down there. They beat him up pretty good."

Beside her, Vicktor said nothing.

Finally, "And Josh?" Bless him for asking. Because he knew she wouldn't leave without her nephew. Which meant that Vicktor would do anything it took to get him out alive. He was that kind of friend.

"I haven't seen him. Darya thinks he's being held in the same prison as Chet."

Vicktor lowered the glasses. "How many men in the camp?"

"Three hundred, at least. All heavily armed. All on the lookout for a rescue party."

Vicktor turned to her. "Then let's give them one."

"Do you ever think about the things you wish you had done?"

The voice came from across the cell, distracting

Chet from his fight against pure exhaustion. His brain wasn't exactly cooperating as he tried to sort out how he might negotiate Josh's release or, as a last resort, create enough of a distraction to help the kid escape.

He was pinning his hopes on option number one.

Of course, a smart man, one who understood the nuances of international negotiation and security, who, say, ran a business doing exactly that, might have formulated a strategy before leaping full speed ahead into his own demise. Yeah, he was a real genius.

Chet hoped God hadn't given up on him. Because he'd certainly given up on himself.

Josh's words had a ring of regret to them as they drifted across the cell. Chet had used the same tone when he'd told his old partner, David Curtiss, that he was resigning from the military after he'd spent time in the hospital, then in recovery, mulling over all the things he'd sacrificed.

"Yes," Chet said in answer to Josh's question. He let Mae's smile fill his vision, thinking of the way she'd looked at him as she'd hunkered down in the sidecar, her hair streaming out behind her. He thought of their glorious week in Seattle, when he knew he'd never get her out of his system. He wasn't sure why he'd even bothered trying. Yes, he had a list of things he wished he'd done, like marry the woman who knew his dark truths and didn't flinch.

"Me, too," Josh said quietly. "I guess that's why I stuck around here after all my teammates headed stateside. I saw all the work I was leaving behind, and it didn't seem right. Like what I'd done wasn't enough. And of course, Darya was here."

Chet's eye had stopped throbbing, although his nose was still on fire. The bruises simmered on his body. He shifted, wishing he could hear noises outside. From the scrap of night he could see through the slatted window, he knew hours had passed—it was probably past midnight. He hoped Mae was already across the border with Darya.

"I think you did all you could, Josh. You were brave to want to help her." How Chet wished the kid had made it to the border, all the way to Turkey. He closed his eyes against the ironic what-ifs.

"I had a friend this year in school who had leukemia. He died in June. He was only twenty. The worst part is, he didn't want to quit school—despite how much pain he was in, he was determined to finish. He was desperate to hang on to this life. I asked him, once, why he didn't just let go. He told me that the closer he got to heaven, the more he wanted to lean into all God had for him here.

That it was in this harsh, earthly landscape that we understand the meaning of God's grace. He said we don't see the depths and power of grace when life is easy. It's only when things start to fall apart around us, when the road crumbles before us, that we turn to grace for every step."

Josh's voice fell, so low Chet could barely hear his words. "He said he was the lucky one, because he'd learned not only how to hold on to God. He'd learned that God was holding on to him."

Hold on.

The voice thrummed through him, separate from his thoughts. *Hold on.*

He could hold on to Mae and the knowledge of his beautiful daughter. And he'd hold on to his friendships with Vicktor and David. And the company he'd started that protected people like little Gretchen, even if he had to dress in tulle to do it. Yes, and he'd even hold on to his memories of Carissa.

"What are you going to do when we get out of here, Josh?" Chet said, keeping his voice even.

"I don't know. Maybe I'll be a missionary. Or... what do you do?"

Chet smiled. "I protect princesses, and sometimes save the world."

"That sounds like a job description I might like."

Footsteps slapped against the cement hallway outside. Chet listened for voices, for movement outside.

Nothing.

Then a key banged in the heavy door, clicking the lock. Like an exhalation, the door eased open, whining on its hinges.

Chet tried to ready himself for whatever was coming, his heart pounding in his chest. Josh jumped to his feet and moved to help Chet stand.

A light flashed, first over Josh, who flung up his hand in recoil, then on Chet. He flinched.

Then darkness turned to light. "Time to go, sir," said Wick.

FIFTEEN

What was taking them so long? Mae sat in the prince's darkened helo, ready to fire it up as soon as Artyom gave the all-clear. She could barely make him out in his recon position inside the ring of darkness outside Bashim's private quarters, well-concealed from the sight of the prison sentries. She did, however, have a clear view of Bashim reclining at his table inside, gorging himself on Moldavian wine and lamb, treating his Iranian grandson-in-law-to-be to a lavish feast.

With his prize possession—his beautiful grand-daughter—serving her betrothed.

Darya had already delivered a tray of what looked like lamb kebobs, a new, red hijab wrapped around her head and wearing a flowing green dress that made her appear every inch the princess Akif claimed she was.

She'd done it. Marched right back to camp, knocked on the doors and swept back into her grandfather's arms without flinching. Mae wasn't sure what words had passed between them behind the scenes—Darya hadn't uttered a sound when she'd let Mae in through the back gate.

Nor when she'd seen Vicktor, Wick, Dekker and Artyom.

But she had smiled.

Now Mae sat in the quiet chopper, her heart hammering its way up her throat. Too long. What was taking them so long? All they had to do was get inside the prison, find Chet and Josh and…what if Chet was so hurt he couldn't move? What if—

Nope. She wasn't going there. She wasn't going to let her fears immobilize her.

Movement flickered near the back of the prison. It wasn't one of Chet's men. This guy wore a blue shirt and slung an older-looking Kalashnikov across his chest. He walked right into the spotlight without a care of concealment, right toward the door where Wick—

"Perestan!"

Stop! Oh, no, he'd seen something, and Mae winced as he aimed his weapon into the night. A shot. Barreling out of the chopper, Mae lunged toward the guard as he yelled again. She took him down before he managed another shot, hitting him in the back with both arms crossed, sweeping his feet out from under him. She landed with her knee in his spine, twisting his arm back in a submission hold.

Then she looked up.

Dekker stood there, breathing hard, mouth slightly agape. "Remind me not to get in your way. You're a little scary."

"Did you find him?"

"Aunt Mae." Josh appeared, white-faced, looking pretty good for having spent three days on the run, and one night in Akif's tombs.

"Joshy!"

Dekker disarmed Mae's captive, shoving his weapon against his neck. And then she had her arms around Josh, holding him tight, just like she did when he was little, squeezing him hard. "Are you hurt?"

"Not yet."

"Okay." She let go of him and forced herself to get moving. She'd check for injuries later. And that was when the grilling would start.

"Where's Chet?"

The words had barely left her mouth when Vicktor appeared, bearing the weight of another man.

Chet.

Or what was left of him. Mae forced herself not to gasp or cry out. He looked as if he'd been hit by a tank, both eyes nearly swollen shut, stumbling badly as they pulled him over the threshold. "Get moving, Mae," Vicktor said, probably to keep her from dissolving.

She turned. The chopper. *Get to the chopper.*

But what about Darya…

"Where's Darya? We can't leave her," Josh said, on the track of Mae's thoughts.

Chet's head lifted. He may have tried to meet Mae's eyes, but in the darkness, she wasn't sure. She grabbed Josh's arm. "She's coming."

Please, Darya, for Chet's sake…for Josh's sake…

They hightailed it to the chopper, Chet staggering, Luke blocking and—

Light exploded around them, floodlights laying them bare. Dekker kept running as a shot from behind them cracked the air.

"Take cover!" Vicktor yelled, and he and Wick returned fire.

Another shot crumpled Dekker right before her eyes. He lay, writhing in the dirt, the chopper some twenty feet away.

She grabbed Josh and beelined behind a bulwark of barrels. Oh, perfect, she'd picked a barrel of gas to hide behind. Vicktor had chosen slightly more wisely, behind a truck. Out in the open, Dekker curled into a ball, clearly trying to stifle his pain.

"Stop." The voice, dark and resonant, issued

from a large man who walked out followed by a horde of soldiers. He appeared red-eyed and soused, unsteady on his feet, which made him even more dangerous.

Akif Bashim.

"Stop. I only want Pancho. The rest can leave."

The rest can leave. Mae shot a look at Vicktor, who was having a bit of trouble holding Chet down. Clearly Pancho was ready to acquiesce. *No, please, Vicktor, don't let him.*

Chet got a few words out, despite the hand Wick locked over his mouth. "I surrender—"

Wick levered him to the ground, and Chet clearly didn't have the strength to resist.

"We're not leaving without him. Sorry," Vicktor said, in calm Russian.

"Let them go, Grandfather."

Everyone froze. Josh went wide-eyed as Darya walked up from behind them. She still wore her beautiful green dress and the decorative hijab. But over it, she wore Josh's jacket, which bore the emblem of the Arizona Wildcats.

"Let them go, Akif."

"You go back to the house. Your fiancé is waiting."

"I will. Right after you let them go." Her eyes panned toward the chopper, as if searching for Josh, or maybe Chet.

"What is she doing?" Next to Mae, Josh had started to fidget, ready to leap up and make a run for her. Mae put her hand on his arm and clamped tight.

"I can't do that, Darya," Akif said. "You know what he did. He must pay—"

"No, Grandfather. He's paid enough. Let him go, and I will stay."

"No!"

Mae squeezed Josh's arm, but the outcry could just as easily have issued from Chet, who'd come alive again. Of course.

"Darya—"

And then Darya opened the jacket. Mae went cold, and next to her, Josh stilled. Even Wick stopped restraining Chet for a moment.

Only Dekker's groans broke the silence.

Darya had strapped to her body a vest wired with enough ammo to take out half of Bashim's camp, and maybe even their group, too.

Not to mention, of course, Darya herself.

"She can't be serious," Josh said, his lips hardly moving, his voice thin.

"She looks serious to me."

Darya held up a detonator in her hand, her thumb poised over the trigger. And, as if to scatter any remaining doubt, she added, "I've been paying attention, Grandfather, to everything you've every said. Including how to arm a bomb."

Next to her, Josh let out a cry that wrenched Mae's heart. "I'll do it, Grandfather. I'll do it unless you let Chet, Josh and their friends go." Then she turned toward the chopper and said, "And, Josh, if you love me, you'll get my father, and Mae, and leave. Now. And don't look back."

Akif looked as if his head might explode. He stared at her, eyes red, face hot, shaking, and Mae had no doubt that watching his financial bargaining chip threatening to blow herself into tiny unmarketable bits had turned him stone-cold sober.

That was what happened when you treated someone like a commodity.

But Josh, who most certainly hadn't treated Darya like a commodity, wasn't holding it together any better. Mae now had both arms around him, hissing into his ear. "She's doing this for you, Josh. You gotta let her do it."

He thrashed in her arms, elbowing her hard, but she held on, despite the catch of her breath.

"Let me go!"

His tone broke her heart, but she dug her feet in. "Do you want to get her killed?"

He shook in her arms, his breath coming fast.

Clearly, no one wanted to see Darya make good

on her threat. Mae shot a look at Vicktor, who was doing the quick math.

They could protest—tell Darya they weren't moving—and risk her making good on her threats.

Or they could go, and return for her another day.

Josh pushed Mae's arms away from him, and she let go, grabbing his wrist. "C'mon. You need to trust her."

Tears cut down Josh's face as he stood. He stared at Darya with a look that broke Mae nearly in half. She stared back at him, her dark blue eyes fierce.

I love you.

He mouthed it, but Mae heard it loud and clear.

Then, lips drawn tight into a grim line, he turned and ran toward the chopper.

"The helicopter!" Akif yelled from behind them, but Mae didn't turn to look. He wouldn't choose the chopper over his granddaughter…

No one was sticking around to find out. Vicktor and Wick wrestled Chet toward the chopper. They loaded him in, and Vicktor held him down while Wick went back for Dekker. It looked as if he'd been shot in the leg. His face was a mask of pain as he stumbled toward the chopper.

Which Mae already had fired up, the blades rotating into a whir, sifting up dust, throwing it on Bashim's army.

And in the center, holding her arms high, stood Darya, tears dripping off her chin, eyes fixed on the chopper. Probably on Josh, but maybe also on Chet, who had stopped struggling and now simply stared at his daughter, an unrecognizable expression on his mangled face.

Mae couldn't watch. Not only because she was trying to lift an Mi-17 off the ground, but because she understood. Truly, finally got it.

Doomed.

Because when you loved someone, really loved them, you had to let them make their own choices. Even if you hated it. Even if it cost you so much of yourself that you wondered if there would be anything left.

You didn't have *doomed,* until you first had *loved.*

Chet would live. Josh would live. Because Darya had loved them enough to let them go.

As they lifted away, out of the wash of floodlights and into the night, she looked down and saw Darya smile up at them and wave.

"You don't look so good."

The voice roused him, and for a second, Chet

thought he was back in the dank cell with Josh, testing his pain as he forced his eyes open.

Oh. Not in a prison cell, his body pressed into the concrete floor, bleeding out, but in a bed. A soft bed, with Mae smiling down at him, fatigue around her eyes. "You Lunds have terrible bedside manners," he said through parched lips.

Mae lifted a plastic cup and angled a straw toward him. "You think *we* have bad bedside manners? This morning, you called me David and told me I needed a haircut."

He took a sip of the water and swallowed it slowly, letting it moisten his throat. "This morning?"

"I forgive you on account of the fact that you were probably high. You've got two broken ribs and a bruised kidney. You're lucky to be alive." She ran her fingers lightly down his face.

"Where am I?"

"A hospital in Prague. We didn't want to take any chances."

He vaguely remembered a choppy, cold ride in the back of an army cargo plane. "When did we get here?"

"Early this morning."

He'd been out of it for a while. Night panned the window, a few bright lights indicating the city beyond the glass.

Then it came back to him, watching his daughter surrounded by terrorists as the darkness clipped her out of his view.

He reached up, despite the IV attached to his arm, and caught Mae's hand. "Darya. Was I dreaming, or did she stay behind, with a suicide vest strapped to her body?"

He kept seeing that image over and over again, punching through the waves of black. Each time he broke free, slicked in a cold sweat, it snared him again. "Please, tell me that was a nightmare."

Mae wore a grim expression. "No, I'm afraid that wasn't a nightmare."

He closed his eyes, wincing as breath raked through his chest. He didn't recognize the sound that emanated from him.

Mae squeezed his hand. "She's going to be okay, Chet."

Yeah, like Carissa had been okay. Trapped in a life she hadn't deserved. "We have to get her out."

"Maybe. But I met an interesting guy out in the hallway. Big, blond. He says to tell you that you did a good job."

As if on cue, the door opened, and Miller walked into the room.

Ole Miss. Chet gave him his best turn-to-ash glare. The agent looked unfazed as he reached into his pocket and pulled out a card. He took one look at Chet's hand clasped over Mae's and handed her the card. "Nice talking to you, Miss Lund. If you ever need anything…"

Mae took the card and gave him a nod.

What?

"As for you, Mr. Stryker, the agency thanks you for your work. And of course would appreciate your silence on the matter."

"I want to know when we're getting Darya out of there."

Miller glanced at Mae. "She hasn't filled you in, then."

Mae tightened her grip on his hand when she said, "Darya is already in Iran. The wedding is in a week. And the CIA has no intention of stopping it."

Chet could feel the roar coming out of him as he sat up, even as his ribs screamed at the effort. "What? You're going to let her marry—"

"Yes, we are."

"Calm down, Chet." Mae pressed her hand on his chest. "First, you need to remember that marrying Akeem was Darya's idea. They're friends from London. She's even fond of him. But most of all, she wants to do this."

"She's just a kid!"

"She's older than most kids her age." Mae

glanced at Miller, then back at Chet. "I think you should listen to what he has to say." The look in her eyes suggested there was more to the story.

"We've got a man inside her house. An Iranian who will keep his eye on her. And I promise, if we get so much as a whiff that she's in trouble, we'll yank her out of there."

Chet lay back, his gaze scanning from Mae to Miller and back.

"You're just going to have to trust her, Chet," Mae said softly.

"She's a kid."

"She's an adult. And she's made her own decision." She leaned close, her lips brushing against his ear. "She did it for you, Chet. Let her."

Chet closed his eyes. *Let her.*

That was the hardest part, wasn't it? Living with the decisions of others.

Or even your own.

Mae's hand found his again, and squeezed.

Chet opened his eyes and met Miller's. "I want updates. And an immediate phone call if anything—and I'm talking so much as a hang-nail—happens to her. I hate this. You should know that."

The agent seemed to sense there might be more behind Chet's tone, because he gave him a tight nod.

The door swished softly behind him as he left. Mae put her chin on their clasped hands. "You going to be okay?"

He looked away, toward the curtained windows. "No. But what choice do I have?"

Mae ran her thumb over his hand. "She's smart. And brave. Just like her father."

"No, she's a thousand times better than her father."

Mae smiled. "Yeah, maybe. But she got it all from you."

No, she'd gotten at least half of it from Carissa. "I don't know how I'm supposed to stay sane with women like her, and you, in my life."

He managed a slight smile. She didn't match it.

"What?"

"I'm just glad you're alive." Moisture formed along her lower lid. He reached out to catch a tear as it spilled over. "I understand now."

He ran a finger down her cheek. "Understand what?"

"Doomed. I understand *doomed*."

"I was wrong, Mae. I'm not doomed. I'm… rescued. When I'm with you, I'm rescued from everything else. In fact, I'm flying. So I guess I can afford a little panic once in a while."

"Chet, I don't have to fly for you. I understand…I

understand your fear. I mean, I thought I was going to lose it when I saw them carry you out of the prison. I never, ever want to go through that again. So, really, I understand if you don't want me to fly for your—"

"Stop. Of course you have to fly for me. You're the best pilot on two continents. Sure, you take risks—probably too many—but that's what I need. Someone who isn't afraid to do what it takes to get the job done. You're the perfect pilot for Stryker International."

"Really?"

"Well, actually, no."

She stared at him, a look of confusion on her face. So he smiled.

"You're the perfect woman. For me. I love you, Mae. I should have never let you walk out of my life. But I know, too, that I need to let you make your own decisions. Because I do respect you. And I trust you. Most of all, I'm tired of walking around in this no-man's-land of needing you, not having you, being scared of letting you too close, being afraid you'll go too far. But it's time to find our place. The place we *both* belong."

She looked so beautiful, a smile playing on her face, her red hair tumbling around her shoulders. He wrapped his hand around her neck and pulled her close.

"Chet, you're hurt."

"Not that hurt."

Then he kissed her, and she was so gentle, so sweet as she touched her lips to his, and he wanted more.

"Marry me, Mae. In Prague or Seattle. Wherever. Because when I'm with you, I'm home."

She pulled back, her eyes on his. A smile creased her face, one that could probably heal him on the spot. "Not Seattle. Please, not Seattle."

"Is that a yes?" he asked.

She nodded. "I knew you needed me."

"I suppose this is where I admit that you're right." He pulled her close, her lips a breath from his. "I can't live without you."

She skimmed her lips against his, then leaned in to his ear. "It's about time, Chet Stryker. It's about time."

He leaned back into his pillow. "If I close my eyes…you'll still be here when I open them again, right?"

She smoothed his hair back from his face, kissed his forehead. "I'm not going anywhere, tough guy. Ever."

* * * * *

Dear Reader,

When my son went to China as a missionary the summer of 2008, he called me from LAX, around midnight. "See you in two months!"

The words echoed in through my heart. What if something happened to him in China? His mother would most definitely go to the rescue (with a guy like Chet!). Right then, a story emerged.

I love Chet because he struggles with his mistakes. Just like Jacob, who wrestled with God on his return to the place of his sins (*Genesis* 32). Chet wants to be forgiven, but doesn't know how to hold on to grace. When God returns him to the land of failure, He sets Chet free, just as He did Jacob.

God longs to help us hold on to grace and set us free, too. It's a matter of wrestling with our faith—and yes, sometimes we are wounded—but believing in God's blessing.

Susan May Warren

QUESTIONS FOR DISCUSSION

1. At the beginning of the story, Mae longs to fly for Stryker International. Unfortunately, her dreams are dashed. Have you ever longed for something that didn't work out? What was it, and how did it make you feel? Could you relate to Mae?

2. Chet has a literal wound—from being shot in a previous book, *Wiser than Serpents*—but he also has an emotional wound. What is it? How does that affect his relationship with Mae? Do you have any wounds from the past that affect your current relationships?

3. What compels Mae to go to the Republic of Georgia? Have you ever traveled overseas? Where have you gone, and have you ever been afraid while you were there? Why?

4. Chet returns to a land where there is a "price on his head." Why? Have you ever returned or gone someplace where you were considered the enemy? How did that make you feel?

5. How does Mae feel about Chet coming to Georgia to assist her? Have you ever been

forced to work with someone who hurt you or whom you disliked? How did you handle it?

6. Mae and Chet travel through a war-torn area—one that is on the edge of violence. Have you ever been in a place that has recently experienced a violent event? How did that make you feel?

7. After Mae and Chet jump off the train, Mae breaks down, frustrated that although she seems to do everything "right," God doesn't seem to be on her side. Do you ever feel this way?

8. Josh and Darya have run away "because of love." Have you ever done something "stupid" in the name of "true love"?

9. Chet makes a decision to surrender to the rebels. Then, Darya makes a courageous act to save her father and his friends. Do you think you could have done what Darya or Chet did? Have you ever made a sacrificial act for the good of a larger group?

10. What realization does Chet have that allows him to commit to a relationship with Mae? Do you agree with his thinking?

11. Chet tells Mae numerous times (and then himself) to hang on to grace. What do you think that means? How have you held on to grace in your life? Give examples.

LARGER-PRINT BOOKS!

**GET 2 FREE
LARGER-PRINT NOVELS
PLUS 2 FREE
MYSTERY GIFTS**

Love Inspired®
SUSPENSE
RIVETING INSPIRATIONAL ROMANCE

Larger-print novels are now available...

LARGER-PRINT BOOKS!

**GET 2 FREE
LARGER-PRINT NOVELS
PLUS 2 FREE
MYSTERY GIFTS**

Love Inspired®

Larger-print novels are now available...

LILP10R